God's Day Off

by Jon Amels

Jon Amels © Copyright 2006

All rights reserved

No parts of this publication may be reproduced, stored in a retrieval system, or transmitted in any form or by any means, electronic, mechanical, photocopying, recording or otherwise without the prior permission of the copyright owner.

British Library Cataloguing In Publication Data
A Record of this Publication is available
from the British Library

ISBN 1846851718
978-1-84685-171-1

First Published May 2006 by

Exposure Publishing, an imprint of Diggory Press,
Three Rivers, Minions, Liskeard, Cornwall, PL14 5LE, UK
WWW.DIGGORYPRESS.COM

CHAPTER ONE

DAYS OF REST

monday

In the beginning Godfrey dug a hole and put in the pond liner. On the second day he added the waters. On the third day he brought forth the plants. The two great lights were set up to give light upon the pond and they were lit in the evening of the fourth day. The fish were then bought and set free in the pond and Godfrey said it was good. He wanted them to be fruitful and to multiply. This is what happened on the fifth day. Godfrey said, 'let the pond bring forth frogs and newts and mosquitoes and bugs'. When it was done, he looked into the surface of the water and saw his own image reflected back. This was the morning and the evening of the sixth day. On the seventh day Godfrey left the pond to its own devices and flew to Italy with his family for a two-week holiday.

Until the flight out, my greatest theological worry had been whether or not I would say, in my dying breath, 'Dear God, please forgive me for all my sins and accept me into the Kingdom of Heaven' or 'Oh, shit!' as the cause of my demise hit me.

I looked at the pleasing body of a young woman as she stood on the beach. After a while she picked up a T-shirt and pulled it on, covering her bosom. She bent to find a bottle of water in her bag. I found myself peering to see her chest, now mostly hidden. I caught sight of one of her nipples. Even though her breasts had been on full display a few moments earlier, I found that brief glimpse extremely erotic.

Why was this more interesting than seeing her when she was fully exposed? Was it because I was not supposed to see something that had become private? Was Eve even sexier when she wore her fig leaf and Adam saw the occasional glimpse of her pubic hair? Was it because I had broken a taboo by looking at the prohibited?

Was this the great meaning of life? Wanting to see what is hidden and forbidden for our own pleasure and amusement? Taking from the universe what is not ours to steal? Having the power not to be punished for breaking the rules? Hoping to glimpse the great secrets of our existence? Wanting to read the last page to see 'who-dun-it' and why?

Perhaps it is the nature of all men to be voyeurs. Maybe it is our curiosity that has driven us for the tens of thousands of years we have survived, rather than lust. This soft-bodied animal without claws, fangs or scaly armour has been able to dominate the fish, birds and every living thing in the world.

The original sin of eating from the tree of life, committed so far back in time by the primal dysfunctional family, had caused the vandalism of everything that God had created. Dominion and jurisdiction have become domination and destruction.

'Bollocks! Why should I pay for what they did?' I muttered.

'Who has done what?' Miriam replied.

'Sorry. I was dreaming.' This was an easier answer than explaining my wandering thoughts.

'More like fantasising. I saw you looking at that girl.' At least Miriam was smiling. She was tolerant, sometimes.

I was taking a holiday with my family. I needed to get away from the pressure of my bank chasing me to pay off my overdraft caused by the need to pay my tax bill. Those two conglomerates conspired to make sure that the money that I earned was never mine. Water charges, rates, gas and electricity bills, office rent and telephone charges took other big chunks. Everyday, I wondered why I only seemed to work to pay the big salaries of corporate high flyers and Civil Servants. I wanted to be free of pressure for just two weeks of the forty eighth year of my existence.

On the plane I had met a man who became a catalyst for a change in my whole perspective of life.

'Hello. My name is Annan Singh.' The old man reached his hand over the middle seat for me to shake.

'Hi. My name is Godfrey Rendell, but most people just call me Gee. God is a bit strange as a short name and Frey suggests that I do not charge.' After this often-repeated introduction of my name I shook his hand and then looked away in order to avoid eye contact. Occasionally, meeting people on a flight is a useful way to pass some time. More often than not, it is annoying. Maybe, if my fellow passenger had been a young lady, I would have found more enthusiasm to talk.

The man was quiet for perhaps thirty seconds. He had a quizzical look on his face. Then his eyebrows lifted as if he had found an answer.

'Where are you going?' He asked.

Why do people ask such stupid questions? We were on a Boeing 737 that was flying directly to Venice. Where else could I be going but there?

'Venice.' I replied curtly.

'I know that.' He chuckled. 'Where are you going after we land?'

He was not letting me go easily.

'We are going to the coast for a holiday.'

His eyes scanned my wife and our two teenage sons who were sitting on the other side of the aisle. He must have noticed that I had been chatting to them and he made his assumptions.

'Nice family.' He nodded his approval of my choice of companions.

'Yes.' I tried to end the conversation by picking up a copy of the in-flight magazine from the pocket on the seat in front. He fell silent.

A little later I turned to look at this man who had been so obviously desperate to have a conversation with me. He was in his late sixties, I guessed. His appearance was Asian but his clothes were Western. He wore a brown mohair jacket that would have cost more than I earned in a month. His head and body were those of a thin Buddha. He smiled at me, the curving lines of his face extending the look of contentment away from his lips to cover his whole face.

I started to feel guilty. This man seemed to be on his own and he was probably lonely. Maybe he worried about flying and wanted to distract his mind. He seemed to allow my evaluation and then pounced.

'So what do you do for a living, Gee?' It was if a trap had been baited and sprung.

Despite being worried that he would try to sell me life insurance or a car, I told him.

'I'm a clinical psychologist.' Often, that would intimidate people into distancing themselves from me. They worried that I would be able to see inside their minds and detect every guilty thought and deed that they had participated in.

'I'm a retired businessman. I'm going back to India to visit my family and to die in good time. I'm an old Indian from New Delhi. Get it?' He chuckled.

I put the magazine back into the seat in front of me and turned to face this man. I had decided that he might be interesting to chat with for a while. He obviously had a sense of humour and jokes were few and far between in my profession.

'Why did you say that you are going back to die? Are you not well?'

'I said I'm going back to die, but I didn't say that I'm planning to do that soon. I know where I will die but I have no idea what happens afterwards. I reckon if we were all sure that Heaven was our destination then we would all kill ourselves. Perhaps the lemmings know more than us.' He laughed, paused and continued. 'No, I just want to find a simpler way to live my remaining life in a more civilised world than America or England.'

I was surprised.

'But those places are civilised. Needs are taken care of, people don't starve. Those places have good healthcare.' I was a bit worried that I was giving away my stereotypical view of India as a backward place.

Undeterred, Annan continued his questioning. 'Where do you practice your profession of psychiatry?'

'Clinical psychology.' I corrected, and then added, 'Guildford.'

The eyebrows lifted again, but just for a fleeting moment.

'OK. A clinical psychologist. You must have dealt with the inner nature of people over your years of experience. You have seen bad behaviours that you have described as primitive.'

'Yes.' I replied, 'Civilisation is only a thin veneer over the primal nature of men. Scratch that surface and you find animals and savages underneath.' My point was made.

'How wrong you are.' His smile diluted the effect of his professional slur. 'When we say that men revert to animal ways, we insult animals. The primal drives that we have are gentle, peaceful and caring. It is so called civilisation that has developed the characteristics that are anything but animal. Think about it. Just because a lot of humans can read and write we assume that we have culture. We then assume that culture is a sign of civilisation. The Renaissance followed one of the most troubled periods in European history, the Black Death.

'However, from that came great works of art in Italy and France, one of the signs of what you call civilisation. That was the birth of the Reformation, when the church tried to clean up its act. And yet, the history of Switzerland has been untroubled by the destruction of war. All it has managed to create is the cuckoo-clock.' He laughed. 'Sorry. That is a very old joke.'

I was silenced by this verbal typhoon.

Encouraged by the look of bewilderment on my face, he continued.

'God is said to have created everything in six days. He is said to have rested on the seventh. These times are metaphors for aeons. If I suggested that the seventh day is still happening, and that God is still resting, could you follow my argument that man has set his heart on destroying everything that was created while God's back is turned? There are only two outcomes. Either the world, and its life, will be killed before God comes back, very angry, on Monday morning, or we will decide to clear up the mess that we have made before we get into deep trouble. I propose to you that civilisation is a euphemism for the more sophisticated ways in which we can destroy each other and the contents of our planet for selfish, personal gain.'

I scanned my knowledge for signs of mental illness. I was worried that he would try to high-jack our aircraft. He did not relent. It was as if he had found an audience that could not escape. He must have been allowing these thoughts to fester like a sore in his head.

'I was born a Sikh in India, but I was educated at an English school which taught me Christianity. When you look at religions they all end up the same. The principle is that there is one Supreme Being. So why do they all compete? If there is one God with one set of values, it is only the selfish interests of men that make them different. Commands are given. "Go to church; give money. Go to the temple; give money." Men sell solutions to the problems that they create. If you do so-and-so, then you will go to whichever Heaven is being offered by the seller you are listening to. Faith becomes nothing more than dogma.'

I tried to interrupt, but he was unstoppable.

'If you live a life according to the rules of the church then you will get a better seat in Paradise. How can the Creator be so conditional? Surely there is a difference between spirituality and religion. One is about the essence of life; the other is about the power of control by men.

'I think men are like children. If they cannot have complete possession of a toy then they will break it to prevent their brother from playing with it. Men have become jealous of the creative power of God, and they want to destroy His masterpiece. Think about it, my friend. Maybe, just maybe, there is no battle between good and evil, but rather a war between the spirit of all life on earth and a God made in the image of man. What became of Zeus?' He seemed to finish.

'I hope I am not offending you.' He added as a closing get-out clause whilst smiling coyly.

This man was not a priest, missionary or New Age guru. He was something else that I did not yet recognise and I was sure he had a psychosis that I had failed to diagnose.

The plane bumped onto the runway. Our conversation ended with a shake of our hands. I watched as he collected his travel bag from the overhead locker. I could see as he reached up that he was stronger than his years would suggest. He obviously looked after his body. He was gone before the four of us had made it to the door. He was not at the baggage carousel. He had vanished.

'Who were you talking to?' Miriam enquired.

'I don't know.' I replied honestly. 'But he has some major problems. He had more than verbal diarrhoea, it was dysentery. Let's get our bags and head for the bus.'

As we got to the outside of the airport, I saw Annan close up his cell phone and climb into a car that was waiting for him.

Italy in July is only a 'cool' place for young people. For the rest of us it is hot. We had to take two buses to get to the camping site. Even though they were air-conditioned, the heat from the crush of human bodies was intense. I did my best to distract myself from the discomfort by looking at the flat landscape that had been reclaimed from the sea by Mussolini. Even bad men could be constructive. Yet, the buildings were empty. They stood at the edge of the road as monuments to the urbanisation that was a hallmark of modern life. The countryside had been abandoned. We are drawn to buy holiday retreats in the rural parts of Italy and France but the irony is that we need to work in towns to pay for them.

I managed to tell Miriam about the strange man who had accosted me on the outward journey. She was intrigued by what I recalled from Annan's hypothesis about the primal nature of modern mankind but we chatted more about our destination.

We were on our way to a rented caravan on the Adriatic coast. We would live the next two weeks of our lives in a small and hot piece of tin, but we would be close to a beach, some shops and Venice. Holidays should offer change and the opportunity to relax.

'The boys will sleep in the awning and we will be in the van.' Miriam informed me as if she was a package tour guide. She looked tired and in need of a break away from her office. Now in her late forties, she still looked as good and fresh to me as when I had first met her many years before. Her dark hair, now helped by a regular application of henna, still eased its way down to her shoulders in loose curls that were fun to stroke.

Our two sons had the tallness of their mother and were developing into handsome young men who would use their looks to charm many girls when they found the confidence to talk to them.

Eventually we arrived at the camping site, tired and sweating. We checked in as if we were registering at a high security compound. The receptionist even kept our passports. We then made our way to the caravan that would be our home for the next two weeks.

We walked down orderly avenues of mobile homes. Some were less mobile than others and had little gardens neatly planted out. On each side of the roads, caravans and camper vans faced their opposite numbers. At a discreet distance to the rear, other retreats from modern life adorned their own pathways. Tall trees made screens between the roads and, as we discovered later, served as high-rise apartments for mosquitoes.

Our caravan was compact but the awning made more room. Luckily, we faced a hedge so we did not have to look at other holidaymakers. To the right of the van there was an area for the table with four chairs that would be our open-air dining room. At the front, the awning was a reasonably large extension. There was space for the two lounger chairs and the pair of camping beds once we had unlocked, or rather unzipped, its canvass front door. Thankfully, the entrance to the caravan needed a key.

The smells of food being cooked in the nearby restaurants were powerful, but the aromas of Italy were missing from the inside of our van. It was so clean and shiny that it could have been on the South Coast of England. I had expected the aromas of garlic, herbs and tomatoes. Instead the scent of furniture polish was dominant.

We followed our written instructions about how to connect the electricity, turn on the gas and fill the water barrel. We were turning this can into a modern house. The bedding was set out and the plastic table and chairs carried into the open space that would be our dining room. Eating alfresco, as it is called. Why not call it eating in full view of everybody? I guessed that a foreign word made it sound more exotic and exiting.

We met the people who were on the adjoining plot, a middle aged German couple who spoke some English. My German was rusty and I knew that I would make horrible mistakes if I tried to impress. 'How do you do it with your wife?' or 'What time do you invade the beach?' instead of polite conversation.

The problem with attempting to speak in a different language is that it sounds fine to the speaker but odd to the listener. As if to prove my point, our neighbour told me that 'Mein vife puts up mit mein yawning.'

'Are you tired? I asked.

'Nein. Mein caravan yawning. She up puts it.'

I looked to see the poor lady struggling with guy ropes and a mass of aluminium poles. I smiled and started to move away, reluctant to offer my help. Once again that terrible thought hit me. Had she been in her mid twenties then I would have offered my skills, deficient as they are. What makes us men think that we are able to offer anything to young women? All we want is to be paid attention by somebody who would otherwise ignore us, as I had ignored the need for help from my new neighbour and had attempted to disregard the old man on the plane.

Shortly afterwards, we made a visit to the shops to buy some food, water and wine, those staples of life. The fragrance of fruit and vegetables seduced us to the greengrocers like the songs of sirens. We looked, squeezed and bought. I hate tomatoes, but they tempted me. Apples of love, so I had been told, and I wanted some loving later, keeping the noise from the lads being the only drawback. Aphrodisiacs in healthy food. Wow! We felt like we had discovered the elixir of life. Things in my childhood that were allegedly good for me always tasted foul but here they seemed to have been transformed.

After unpacking, we walked the short distance to the seashore for the first time.

Annan's ideas about contemporary society seemed to have made their home in my perceptions. I found myself in the middle of a multitude of prehistoric natives. Naked children played while their parents relaxed. Bare breasted women moved about, or reclined, on the sand. Men in loin cloths paraded slept or swam. Out to sea, canoes were being paddled in a leisurely way. His words came to my mind. This place was a primeval setting, yet it felt safe.

Nearly naked folk at rest. The clichéd word 'Paradise' emblazoned on a towel summed up the feeling. For two weeks in every fifty two, we find our true, primordial selves. For the other ninety-six percent of the time, we are 'civilised'.

We adopted the dress-code by changing into our swimming costumes shyly behind towels wrapped around our pale bodies. 'Are you going topless?' I asked Miriam.

'Absolutely not. Especially as the boys are here. They would be totally embarrassed. Aren't there enough around for you to look at, anyway. You've seen mine so many times that I thought you would have had enough of them.' Was her less than succinct refusal.

Why was I encouraging my wife to show her breasts to strangers? In our ordinary lives back home, I would have punched a Peeping Tom had he peered through the bedroom window from a mile away. Yet here those things, which all men take full possession of, were able to be exposed to a thousand unknown bags of testosterone with the full compliance of the jealous male.

My strange thoughts were halted by the thump of a beach-ball on my foot. It was time to dive into the water to play with my offspring.

When we returned to the beach we started to build a sand-castle at the edge of the water. Man against nature. We made it taller and higher until we had made a mound that came up to my knees. Then we started to scrape out a moat, piling up more and more sand as we made our defence against the sea. Whereas the Mediterranean is not tidal, further North in the Adriatic, the water rises and falls within a small range. Our battle was to make a secure fortress before the tide made its attack.

The pleasure came from a middle-aged man and two teenagers playing as we all had when they, and I, were small children. The passage of time was slowed for that hour.

As I tried to rub the sand from my hands, I thought about how much human skin was mixed in with the sand following its natural exfoliation of thousands of people during the season. Athlete's Foot, psoriasis, warts and a multitude of other conditions were also at rest over my towel and my body!

We returned to our vantage point to watch nature disassemble our efforts. Miriam was dozing in the bright sunshine. I checked that she was well covered in sun-lotion. She was an attractive sight. She had maintained a good figure and she was, to my mind a younger version of the middle aged woman she now was. She was still nineteen in my mind. I had met old school colleagues at reunions only to be amazed at how old they looked. They were older versions of the images I held in my head. I guess I stopped going to meetings because I needed to retain an image of myself that was different to the reality that they saw.

The boys, young men, were happy kicking the ball around further up the beach. I looked around at the forest of green, red and orange beach umbrellas looking like poisonous mushrooms that had grown tall in the sand. Windsurfers were marooned by the lack of wind. Standing on their boards as if queuing for something, they all appeared to be annoyed that nature had a sense of humour. There had been enough breeze to take them too far out to swim back and then it weakened to leave them in the doldrums. The sight was reminiscent of those documentaries where natives stand in canoes whilst spearing fish.

Settling down on my towel, my thoughts returned to how the World might have been fifty thousand years ago when man was a developing force rather than a dominating one. The balance was different. Like our sand fort, the efforts of people would be eroded and taken away by the strength of nature. Even now those four elements of the Universe are able to dominate. The fire of volcanoes, the water in tidal waves and floods, the earth when split by quakes and the incredible bursts of energy in hurricanes and tornadoes. When these phenomena occurred they would treat concrete and steel with the same scant regard that the waves gave to the sand-castle. The tsunami that happened in Indonesia, the devastation of New Orleans and the earthquakes in Pakistan were major examples. Then, church leaders doubted the existence of God because he had not prevented them, even though they had been brewing for years. Those were the very things that had created oceans and mountains millions of years before. They were the continuing building labourers of our planet. Did the churchmen believe that God should now leave us free from Nature's inherent progress?

Perhaps the first religions came from man's attempts to subdue those monsters. Perhaps from the need to evoke the gentler elements into action. Rain for the crops to grow and sunlight for them to ripen.

Was this the first use of conditional thought and action? 'God of the Heavens, if I do so-and-so, will you please send rain to water my plants? Or keep me safe from disaster? If you do, then I will love and worship you. If you don't then I will doubt you and look elsewhere.'

'Dad, if I promise to do the washing-up tonight, can we go to the Water Park tomorrow?' Mark's voice brought me back to the twenty first century.

Now, I was the arbiter of destiny. I had the choice. 'We will go anyway, but maybe not tomorrow. Let's work out what we want to do later on over dinner.' In this way, perhaps I could negotiate for Nick to offer something as well. Anyway, I hated parks with those adrenaline-evoking waterfalls built in. I wanted to avoid committing too soon.

The sand-castle was still there, but the front had been washed away. 'Why does the sandy beach stay here when structures built on it are eaten away?' My mind refused to think about finding an answer. I fell into a light sleep.

When I woke, I saw a crowd of people staring and pointing at something on the beach at the edge of the water. I got up and walked over to look at whatever was there. Our instinct is to follow the attention of a crowd. The game is played by youngsters on innocent passers-by when they point at nothing in the sky. The joke comes from the others looking in the same direction and not seeing anything. The people just keep on looking. We love control.

This was not a joke. A white, gelatinous dome, the size of a soccer ball, lay on the beach. A jellyfish decorated like a Victorian lady's hat with pretty bows of bright blue around the rim. It was dead. I made a quick visual scan for stinging strings, but there were none. A man pushed and prodded it with a child's spade until it was flipped onto its back. Small cones of jelly flopped over. This creature, blind and unfeeling, was now harmless. My mind lumped it together with the Portuguese Man-of-War with its long poisonous tentacles. Fear is an odd thing. We hear about something that we have never seen and generalise our worries to all members of the same class of creature.

I felt a tap on my shoulder that made me jump. When we are apprehensive, we move into a state of alert.

'Bad sign.'

I turned to see a stranger who needed to talk to anybody who would listen.

'Sorry. Why is it a bad sign?' I asked.

'The increase in their population has been caused by nutrient pollution from the discharges from farming, industry and town wastes. And as a result of over-fishing, jellyfish are increasing in numbers. In the Adriatic, jellyfish have been known to clog fishing nets because they are so numerous.'

He wandered off, shaking his head as he went.

'Nerd.' I thought.

How did he know I was English? Even in swimming trunks we show our nationalities. We carry tribal markings when naked.

We returned to the small area that was defined by our four towels and settled down again. It was shortly afterwards that I saw the topless girl putting on her T-shirt.

After the beach, I showered in the communal block. It was clean. Staff busied around with hoses to ensure that it was kept to a standard set by the owners of the site. As I looked in the mirror to shave, I saw a tired man looking back at me. My blue eyes that I am so proud of were watery. My skin was a little grey to match the hair at my temples. Although I usually felt like an average sort of man, today I was less than that. Maybe the sun had dried my skin. Possibly I was seeing myself as my old school chums had seen me. The joke was that I now saw my father in my own reflection. Thankfully, Miriam liked my dad.

We decided to eat out on that first evening. The site had a wide variety of restaurants that sold the same sort of food. Pizza and pasta dishes abounded. We went to the one that looked the busiest. I like fresh food and a good turnover assured quality in my simple view of cuisine.

We ended our meal and sat to watch the entertainer playing his keyboard and singing a United Nations medley of songs. Italian ballads, German oom-pa-pa and English pop. Perhaps not in a direct reflection of the demographics of the camp inhabitants, but cosmopolitan enough to give that indefinable 'continental' feel.

This man with a bald round head and a corpulent body sang to his keyboard rather than the crowd. There was no applause after his songs, not because he was bad but because he was a human Muzak providing background noise to the constant chatter of the diners. I signalled to Miriam that we would clap at the end of his next song. We did so and others joined in. Like the children who play the pointing game, I love the concept of crowd control. Like sheep, people will follow a lead. Sometimes it had backfired when attempting to give a standing ovation. The rest of the audience will stare at you more than the artist on stage. Anyway, this was not manipulation. It was a show of appreciation. After every song from that point on, the singer was rewarded by soft applause. My job was done.

'Hello. I am Annan. May I join you?' The familiar sing-song tones in the voice alarmed and pleased me at the same time. I was glad he had introduced himself to my family. I had forgotten his name.

'What a small World.' I said, restraining an expletive that would have expressed disappointment.

Annan said, 'Let me get you more wine and we can share a drink.' Without waiting for our comments, he pulled up a spare chair, beckoned a waitress over and gestured that he would like the empty bottle replaced. I was feeling slightly light-headed as we had consumed a few glasses before we had set out for our dinner. I was bemused by the self-assurance of this man.

'Meet my family. I think you saw them on the plane, but you were not introduced.' I turned to my children, and then Miriam, giving her that look that says that I was not happy with this intrusion. 'Annan is the man I met on the plane, yesterday.'

'I am Miriam, Godfrey's wife. I am pleased to meet you. So, are you in a caravan as well?'

'Pleased to meet you.' Annan shook her hand. 'No. I am staying in the hotel. I am getting too old for the camping life.'

'This is Mark.' The tall seventeen year old hid his brown eyes, shook hands and mumbled something, which was presumably polite.

'And this is Nick.' A hand was offered to be gripped and waggled by Annan.

'Nice to meet such fine and good-looking young men.' Annan smiled. He was obviously used to meeting and charming people.

The boys smiled shyly and then mentally withdrew, not sure what to say or do next.

I rescued them. 'Our meetings seem to have been very coincidental. Here we are. Strangers having a drink together when we know very little about each other. So should we first break the ice by saying who and what we are? Do you want to go first?'

The waitress arrived with a new bottle and fresh glasses. We ordered beers for the boys.

'I know what you all are. You are a clinical psychologist, your wife is a beautiful woman and the two young men are at school or college. I think Miriam does not work because she wants to be at home for her children. As for me, I am an old man. Your turn!'

'Hang on.' I frowned in a friendly sort of way. I was perturbed by his reference to my wife. Perhaps he was just a dirty old man after all. 'You said nothing about yourself. We can see that you are a man in his late middle age, but you have said nothing more than is obvious. You described us by what you think we do, but you know nothing about us as individuals.' I chuckled, just enough, to rub away the sharp edges of my tone.

This was going to be boring. This man was going to be vague. He was going to talk in riddles. I was going to be in trouble with Miriam for getting us embroiled in the waste of one of our precious holiday evenings.

'Precisely.' Annan muttered. 'The world is based on what we are rather than who we are. To some, I am a Paki, a turban-head or a terrorist. To others I'm a father, a boss, a friend. To my bank I'm a customer. Does that tell you more about me? No, I guess not. We cannot cope with billions of individuals. We can only manage with generalised stereotypes. The grapes in the wine were grapes. They were Merlot but that's all we know about them as a community. As individuals we know little.'

I felt Miriam's kick under the table. I was in trouble! I was warming to the style of this man, but he was coming over as a lunatic. He was different. The sort of person I would like to meet in different circumstances. Debate and postulation do not mix well with family holidays. Miriam was not a home-maker as speculated by Annan, and she was less than pleased at his generalisation. She worked hard in a small company to help pay the fees of the boarding schools the boys were pupils at.

Annan was wrong. His seemingly wise words were diluted by his narrow-mindedness.

Then he continued. 'So, now let me tell you who you are. You are a clinical psychologist who cares for people. You have insight and compassion. You favour the recovery of your patients above the amount of money that they might pay you if you kept them in therapy for months and years. Your wife works to help pay for the education of her sons. That makes her a concerned and caring person. Now we are talking about qualities of people rather than quantities. Now we are finding out who we are rather than what we are.'

This was the truth about us, but we had not told him. We had only thought it. Perhaps he had read our body language and made his corrections as a result.

The wine was soon drunk and we made our excuses to go. I could see that Miriam was unhappy. I paid the bill including the extra drinks that Annan had ordered for us.

As we were saying our farewells, Annan's phone rang. He spoke in a language that must have been from India, Hindi, I guessed. His pace quickened. He waved goodbye and continued talking into his handset.

Back at the caravan we lit candles and sat outside. The evening was warm and balmy, but I was hot and sweaty! The wine did not help.

The mosquitoes found the garlic and wine mixture that oozed from my pores irresistible. I slapped my face and hands until they glowed red in the dusk. Every so often a bat would swoop past taking its fill.

'We need fewer bugs or more bats.' I complained as much to myself as to the family.

Miriam asked me about Annan.

'You know as much about him as I do. He is not some old buddy that I have bumped into. He is a bloody nuisance who comes at life from a totally different angle. That is the only thing that intrigues me. Maybe I've discovered a new mental condition that encompasses all others. I shall call it Rendell's Complex. No. That makes it sound as if I have it.'

'Let's go to bed.' Miriam's tone was one of escape rather than an invitation to have sex, as difficult as that would be in an oven with our sons on the other side of an open window.

'Why is it so hot?' I moaned.

'Because we're in Italy in the summer. We wanted sunshine and warmth. We've got it. Stop complaining and go to sleep.' Was her reply.

'For God's sake, I only asked.'

As I slipped into sleep, I had a feeling that meeting Annan was one of those coincidences that is more closely related to fate rather than chance.

CHAPTER TWO

THE HAWTHORN BUSH AROUND EDEN

tuesday

The fish pond was quite big. It was large enough to allow plenty of diversity in plant and aquatic life. The fish saw their world for what it was. The sky was the surface of the water. The bottom of the pond was the limit of their planet.

'Sorry, I think I was a bit pissed last night.' My first words of the day were uttered as I pulled on my shorts and headed towards the shop to buy some bread. This was joy for me. Bread that had texture and flavour.

'Give us this day our daily bread.' I always wondered why the word 'please' is not incorporated into the Lord's Prayer. We are conditioned to fear God but we still speak to Him as if He were a servant. Anyway, I returned with my French, or should it be Italian, stick. The boys, lads, or whatever I should call them, were asleep. Miriam was brewing coffee.

'I wonder if we'll meet your guru, Fairy Godmother or Godfather on the beach today. I really need a deep and meaningful session listening to some old weirdo chattering on about modern life!' Miriam's sarcasm was hard to take with my thick head.

'My guru! I hope not. I want to relax as well. Let's get the guys up, fed and watered. Then we can hit the beach. They want to go to the Water Park at some point, but we'll just chill for a few days.'

That was the plan.

By mid-morning, we had carried two umbrellas, two poles, two sun-loungers, four towels, one ball, one Frisbee, two inflatable beds, two litres of water and a bag of assorted sun creams down to our few square feet of sand. Having established camp, we cooled down in the sea.

'How much stuff do we have to transport every day? I feel like a refugee. Carting stuff through sand that burns my feet is not fun.' I felt in rather a good mood as I claimed my space in the shadow of one of the sunshades, scanned our neighbours for exposed body parts and then closed my eyes to the world.

This was a depiction of the grand ideal, the Garden of Eden. My thoughts were running at a rapid rate. Germans, Italians and English folk were sharing a beach that a few decades before they would have been fighting to possess. Free from the competition of Nations and dogma, we all relaxed under the same sun. The power of politicians and churchmen had divided people for thousands of years. Crusaders slayed Saracens. To what end? To satisfy the lust for domination? Men running under the flag of St George. Who was he anyway? A dragon slayer. And what were dragons? They appear in every country's folklore. Perhaps they were representations of volcanoes spewing fire and lava into the air. If so, how did a mounted man with a sword subdue them to the satisfaction of the good folk of the land?

Our ancestors killed in the name of God to spread the commandment 'Thou shalt not kill'. We sanitised the prime sin of homicide for our own sakes. A man is a murderer in peacetime yet a hero when at war. A terrorist is a freedom-fighter when he is on our side. It is acceptable to commit horrors when we are on the winning team.

Yet here, in the campsite, there was peace. By paying rent, we had bought our way through the security system that kept the others out. Genesis says that man was created from dust and then Eden was planted. Adam was put there before being expelled. The cherubim and flaming sword that kept mankind away from the tree of life allowed us in for our two weeks, but we had to remember our passes when we ventured outside the camp or we would be refused readmission.

'Do you want to cool down in the sea?' Miriam's voice brought me back to the beach.

Without answering, I got up and started to walk to the water's edge. The sand was baking hot. At least all those bits of skin would have been sterilised by the heat. The water cooled me as I moved deeper.

We played with each other. Years fell away and we were all babies, innocent and trusting. This was blissful. After a while I floated on my back, relaxing. Every-so-often a wave would lift me up and then gently lower me back down. I felt safe even in this infinite expanse of sea that I was sharing with sharks, giant squids and those Portuguese-Men-Of-War. Who cared? I did not. Those animals only existed in wild-life documentaries and horror films. I had never seen them. I wondered about how much, or little, I knew. If I had never been told anything by other people, how much would I know? I would have to make it up. I would have to invent explanations to satisfy my curiosity. Was that what happened in the early days of mankind?

My thoughts moved back to Genesis, the only chapter of the Bible that I had read more than once. My Religious Studies teacher at school was obsessed by it.

It was as if Genesis is the metaphor for creation and the rest is about men who claimed supernatural powers to subjugate other men. Albeit tongue-in-cheek, I worried that my thinking was blasphemous and that I would be punished. There again, blasphemy was about insulting the God made in man's image, but in my heart I knew that my God was the spirit of life rather than an old man sitting on a gold throne surrounded by sycophants. How could the Creator find enjoyment from an infinite number of people telling Him how great He is all the time? In the great scheme I was pretty unimportant.

Unimportance and insignificance are human conditions that motivate us to rise above our peers. A sense of worthlessness drives us to become rich or famous by whatever means we can.

I had a faith but no religion. I never liked being organised and controlled by others. That is why I enjoyed being my own boss.

I had drifted towards the beach and a breaking wave choked me. I stood up and tried to wipe the salt water from my eyes with my wet hands. Blinded for a few moments, I gradually got my bearings from our two stripy umbrellas.

'Did you have a nice time?' Miriam offered me some water.

'Yes, I did. But my mind seems to be taking me on a trip. You know the expression I sometimes use when my clients let go of their emotional baggage, mental vomiting? Well, I appear to be doing the same thing about religion.'

'Did you find the carrots?' Miriam chuckled. 'There are always bits of carrot in sick, aren't there?'

'Ha, bloody, ha!' I smiled, reached over and gave her a quick kiss on her forehead.

'Thank you, but don't get carried away like that couple in front. Look'. She said.

Between us and the sea I saw a man and a woman face to face, straddling a sun-lounger. They were kissing and caressing each other as if they were in a private room. Oblivious to the mass of sun lovers, he fondled her bare breasts. She kissed him passionately as he continued. After a while I became bored and picked up my notepad. I wanted to jot down my thoughts about creation.

Miriam prodded me and whispered for me to look at a young boy who had planted a small chair at right angles to the couple. He was just a few feet away. He was watching intently. That moment emphasised something for me. Whereas people could be nearly naked on the beach, the place had been sexually innocent until the lovers had brought lust there. They were out of place. They made Paradise a sordid land. They were committing the cardinal sin.

'If they want to screw each other to death, why don't they do it in private?' I complained.

At that point they stood up and, still entwined, made their way into the sea. She appeared to be at least twenty years older than he was and she looked as if she had enough money to keep herself smart and him comfortable. Her hair was well kept and her beach accessories seemed expensive to an everyday chap like me. The man was good looking. His tan was from many days spent on the beach, his physique from a lifetime spent in gyms' and bedrooms, practising his press-ups.

'Gigolo.' I said.

'Lucky woman.' Miriam said with a provocative tone.

A bit later we went for a swim to cool off. The sweethearts were still glued together in the water. My curiosity tempted me to check out whether or not her bikini bottom was on. I could not see without diving impolitely close so I swam away.

When we left the sea and returned to our own space, I whispered to Miriam, 'She's old enough to be his mother.'

'It makes no difference whether a man is older or younger than his mate. I bet you would have enjoyed the comforts of that girl you were ogling yesterday. She is young enough to be your daughter.'

I huffed. The truth has spikes attached to it sometimes.

I then rolled over, and returned to my jotter.

'What do you think God is?' I asked.

'Pardon.' Miriam was dozing.

'Who do you think God is?' I repeated, noticing my own unconscious shift from what to who.

'He's the original super power. He, or She, made the world and its inhabitants and then gave the responsibility for looking after it to men. Thinking about it, He must be a man because a female God wouldn't have trusted men. She would have let women do a better job.'

I ignored Miriam's comment. 'OK. Do you think we are more civilised now than when we were first running around on the plains of Africa?'

Miriam gave me one of her frowns. 'What the hell has got into you, Gee? Are you on some sort of religious trip? You only ever go to church for weddings, Christenings and funerals. I want to sleep. I'm tired. You snored like a pig last night and kept me awake.' She rolled over and shut me out.

'Bollocks.' I mumbled quietly, even though the boys were deafened to outside sounds by earphones plugged into CD players.

I needed to lighten up a bit. I looked at the people on the beach. The arms were away from the body. Legs were spread slightly. With their closed eyes these people were the perfect target for a murderer, rapist, lion or hyena. They were like sleeping dogs and cats. But why? Everybody was a stranger to everybody else. It seemed as if we can only trust those people that we do not know.

I started to write on my pad. "Please indulge me for a while." I did not know why I was apologising to my jotter but continued:

"This predisposition to trust and relax is an example of the primeval innocence that lives in us when we are not threatened. Who threatens? Everybody when organised into a hierarchy. Bosses, corporations, governments, nations and churches. Here we all are, happy to have escaped from our jobs, countries, politicians and civil servants. Perhaps we can relax while vulnerable because there is no power base. It is interesting, however, that there is a multi-denominational church on the camp site. Every-so-often, priests must chat to prospective congregation members. Perhaps the Holy-men need to achieve a good head-count in order to enjoy their own holidays. Pyramids of power are fairly standard in nature. The alpha males and females dominate the subordinate members of their packs. Sophisticated corporate ladders, political corridors of power, Episcopalian principles rule any collection of people within any organisation. The might of weaponry and armies do the same thing amongst nations. Pin-stripes, bishops' robes and atom bombs do not make us more civilised than our ancestors. They had muscles, clubs and stones to wield, but that was more for sex and food than absolute control, I guess. Gorillas behave with a polite sense of violence. Threaten rather than cause bloodshed. And there it is again; who threatens? Everything when organised into a hierarchy. Maybe that is because we want to be at the top. We want to rule the roost. That makes us feel less insignificant than we really are, but the way up is a brutal one. The authors of the Bible told us that God invented the hierarchy by giving man dominion over the other animals and then, Darwin gave the idea credence by showing that we are at the top of the evolutionary ladder. It is ironic that those two ended up working together! For some reason I remember that the cherubim who protect the tree of life from mankind are of the second order of the nine-fold celestial hierarchy of angels. One of those things that we are made to learn at school, but could never comprehend. "

'Shit a brick!' I exclaimed out loud. 'What the hell was going on in the old days of creation in the Bible?'
Miriam looked me as if I had started to fit.

'I reckon that those archaic values have been reapplied. Civilisation started when mankind got its act together after a very brutal and traumatic birth.'

Miriam quickly suggested that we cool off. 'I think that you've had too much sun today. We'll swim and then go back to the van.'

I followed her meekly into the water. Then a mighty cry and a splash that would have made the surfacing of a sperm whale appear quiet, erupted. The Prince of the Marauders had arrived.

This was our affectionate name for Mark. He delighted in scaring people. He had yet to learn that predators never warn their prey of an attack. It happens in cowboy films when warning shots are fired. It happens in horror films when the monsters make eerie sounds. Yet in real life, it never occurs. 'Hello, I am a lion and I am going to chase you after I count from one to ten, out loud.'

Mark did annoy us however, with his violent throwing of water and his attempts to drag his mother under the water.

He is a very likeable young man. He has a sense of shyness that covers his impending mature charm like a bud that is opening. Every-so-often the flower that will be, shows through the adolescent. He is that strange hybrid between man and child with that cocktail of behaviours that youth is cursed with.

Miriam played the game. She pushed him away, pulled him into the foam and threatened him that he would not get an ice cream when the pretty girl with the vending cart arrived later on. This mixture of play fighting and childish menace matched Mark's current state of growth, perfectly. They ended up laughing before a new attack was made on Miriam by Nick.

I sat on my towel and fell asleep. Then I woke screaming, 'I want to go back, now!'

'Have you had enough of the holiday already?' Miriam's voice brought me to full consciousness.

'Shit. I had a nightmare about being dead. I was floating in Heaven with God talking to me about judgement. It was worse than some of the things I have heard in my office. I think I need to talk to my support person when I get back.

Holidays are for relaxation rather than for horror stories. Anyway, who the bloody hell have I upset enough to be punished by becoming dead? God said I have missed happiness on Earth.'

Dreams are so annoying. They tell stories, alter moods and then dissolve away, leaving you with the frustrations of not being able to remember them. Dream recall reminds me of those times when I have tried to pull earthworms from their holes. You get a small grip and then they slip away to hide. Later they might come out fully, but only rarely.

'Shut up Gee. It was a dream, not a real experience. You drank too much last night so it serves you right. It was probably that joint you smoked before we came away. Now, stay awake while I carry on playing with the boys.' Miriam stormed away before I could explain that the 'joint' I smoked was, in fact, made from something I found in the garage which was probably from a stash that belonged to one of her sons. We had long established that whereas her sons always made her proud, mine sometimes transgressed beyond the borders.

The worst thing that a clinical psychologist can do is analyse himself. Like every medical student diagnoses that they have all the terminal diseases going, clinical psychologists decide that they will go crazy. I even had a joke about it. Miriam had said that one day they would take me away. My reply was that it was all part of my retirement plan. Free accommodation and food. My paltry pension would not cope half as well. With any luck and the right chemical input I could spend my last years hallucinating that I was on a planet occupied by Michelle Pfeifer look-alikes.

Miriam seemed to have no interest in my out-of-body experience. Miriam had no wish to listen to the ramblings of my distorted mind, as she put it. All she could say was that with a fat body like mine it would best to be out of it! Jokes reflected her sense of reality, sometimes.

I managed to burn the dinner on the gas grill. Steaks were transmuted into charcoal accompanied with salad and a glass of wine. The boys laughed and Miriam scowled.

Cooking in the open was a competition. My motivation was to waft smells into the campsite air that would make others jealous of what we were going to consume. I had been invaded by fragrances of grilling sausages and pork cutlets, barbequed fish and chicken. I was aware of tomatoes being reduced to a sauce, as the recipe books put it. Smells have an effect on the visual centres of the brain. It is easy to imagine the aromas of food as seen in a cookery book. I could visualise a beautiful bratwurst sitting on a bed of rocket salad, dressed with a fine balsamic vinaigrette. My food was screaming 'I'm burnt. Please help me!' Nobody could sense the salad apart from the vague smell of cat's pee that basil gives off.

I had insisted on cooking so I attempted to move my lack of culinary skills into a witticism. 'It's great to have food that you can write with. This is how art was developed. A cave man who wanted to cook for his loving and grateful family went into his cave and drew the animal that the burnt offering came from with the charcoal made by burning the meat. The first animal to be barbecued was a bison and the first menu card was created all at the same time. The aim is to burn charcoal to ashes and then replace the charcoal with burnt flesh. Next time I will miss out the middleman. I'll serve the fuel straight onto the plate.'

Stony silence followed.

I politely got up from my chair, explained that I needed to be alone for a while, and went to seek out solitude. That was how at the end of my tether I felt.

As soon as I had rounded the corner on my way to the bars, Annan appeared.

'Good evening, Gee. Fancy a drink?' He seemed to be putting on a theatrical Indian accent. He even rolled his head from side to side as if to dress the scene.

I avoided telling him that I was looking for peace and quiet.

We walked to the bar in silence as if walking from a waiting room to the main arena for action. We took our seats and Annan started.

'Gee, you are a troubled man. I can see that. Are your patients getting you down?'

He sounded like me at the start of a session with a client.

'I have clients rather than patients. I am not medically qualified and I do not like to sound pretentious.' I interjected, hoping to balance what was going to be a speech from Annan.

'No matter. But I can see that you are overweight, you smoke and you seem to be anxious. I would like to help you to get better.'

'Are you a therapist or a genie?' I worried that the reference to a genie might be perceived as a racist comment because of his Indian roots.

'I like to help people, that's all. I want to give something back in return for what has been given to me. You have young children and a lovely wife. You should live long enough to enjoy them. Stress kills and you are too young to die.

'Perhaps I am a genie. Ask me for your three wishes.' Annan's smile smoothed my rising hackles.

'OK, I would like more money than I have.'

Annan reached into his pocket and slapped a one Euro coin onto the table. I picked it up and stared at it as if it were a magic trick that was about to happen.

'Put it into your pocket.'

I did.

'Now you have more money than you had. See it works. The sorcery of the genie.' He roared with laughter. I joined in.

'But you will have to pay for our drinks so your extra wealth will be short-lived.' Annan laughed again. I did not see the joke this time, especially as I had paid for his drinks the night before.

'OK. My next wish would be for health and the third wish would be for happiness.' My dreams were clichés, but clichés are those things that are most used, by definition.

'I would ask you to make your first wish for the peace and health of the planet and all its inhabitants. Certainly you should wish for health and happiness for your family and yourself. Those things are far more indispensable than money. But you put wealth before your family. Money kills too many things and having it tends to push health and happiness away. I will help you to gain health. You will be here for the rest of the week so we will start tomorrow on the beach. We need to look at your body, mind and spirit.'

This man should have been running assertiveness training courses. I had no choice but to agree a time and place.

'So how much will this cost me?' I asked. This was usually the first question that I heard from my clients.

'It will cost nothing in money but I will require a favour from you in return.' He answered cryptically.

'What's that?' I wanted to know what I was committing to. I wondered if he wanted to sleep with Miriam, take my boys into slavery or if he wanted me to help him with some crime or other.

He did not answer my question. He just whispered 'trust me'.

We finished our drinks, I paid the bill and we went our separate ways.

'I met Annan in the bar and I've arranged to meet him at ten o'clock on the beach'. I informed Miriam.

She looked surprised. 'So are you two taking a lover's walk in the surf later on?' Her look was half serious.

'Tomorrow morning! We want to talk about getting me a bit healthier than I am. I think he might be some sort of holistic doctor but I can't get any information out of him about himself. It's weird. I called him a genie earlier and he made a joke of it.'

'He probably has less experience of the inside of a bottle than you do.' Miriam quipped as I poured a large glass of wine.

I wondered what the favour that he wanted would be.

CHAPTER THREE

BREATH OF HEAVEN

wednesday

Beyond the sky there were other planets from which aliens would appear. Some were friendly, especially the green aliens that would lay their eggs in huge bundles. These eggs would be offered as food gifts to the fish. The uneaten ones would turn into black wriggly things that swam like fish, but were different. These were good to eat as well.

As we left the caravan after breakfast, we took the same route to the beach as before. Across the dirt track, which passed as a road in front of our caravan, there was a gap in the hedge that zigzagged to avoid a direct line of sight inwards or outwards.

Beyond the hedge we immediately came to a paved area that was also the arena for performances by the itinerant bands of opera and country singers who toured the holiday camping sites. Chairs were being put out for later. The shops were at the end of this square and if we turned right we could wander through a mixture of bars and boutiques. The whole area was a little village at the middle of which traders made their seasonal livings. Again, the feeling of being in a tribal settlement came back. The deep yearnings of modern people for our fountainhead were being satisfied at every level.

We turned left and made our way to the beach. At nine thirty in the morning, areas of sand were already being claimed. Even as temporary settlers, people would return to the same spots everyday, including us. However, even neighbours of a few days would not make any greeting. This was the thing that made the barriers that kept us apart in our innocent states of exposure. Contact is the start of a hierarchy.

We settled down, made the nucleus of our pitch with the umbrellas, and then expanded and protected the zone with towels. This was ours. Our bits and pieces told others to stay away as strongly as the urine signature of a wolf.

Shortly after we had made our camp, Annan arrived. There is a great absurdity in learning something that you have been doing for decades. Annan wanted to teach me how to breathe, but as I might have expected, it was more complicated than that.

'So what is breathing?' He asked.

We made a complementary pair. Annan leaning forward with his eyes open in anticipation of my answer, and me leaning back with my eyes screwed up as if defending myself. I was back at kindergarten.

Being a therapist I knew that deep breathing is important.

'It is what we do to get rid of carbon dioxide and to replace it with oxygen'. My tone was slightly sarcastic, my mood was dark.

Here we were, sitting on towels on a sandy beach early in the morning. Miriam and the boys had decided to go off under the pretext of enquiring about wind-surfing lessons. Yes, I thought! Miriam on a wind-surfer would be like a bishop singing 'gangster-rap'. Possible but unlikely.

'Breathing is life.' Annan started. 'Without breath you would die. In European languages the root word is the Latin 'spirare', to breathe. From that you get words like respiration. But it is also the origin of 'spirit', as in 'inspiration', and more importantly, Holy Spirit. The Romans knew it two thousand years ago. Before that, the Hindi word 'prana' meant the energy of life and breath. Before that the Chinese word 'chi' was used in the same way. Thousands of years ago it was known that breathing and the spirit of life were one and the same thing. We breathe out carbon dioxide and then the trees and plants recycle it to give us oxygen. The cycle of life is a perfect circle, until we chop down all the trees and burn them to make too much carbon dioxide. Civilisation, huh!

'Of course, now, in modern times, we know better! We are taught to breathe badly from childhood by our parents and schoolteachers. '

Annan looked at me and firmly told me to 'Sit up straight.'

I did although I wanted to resist him, even punch him.

How dare he tell me how to sit? Me! A grown man.

He laughed and I became more annoyed. 'See how you obeyed! Those words have been used to train people into being upright and proper. Western culture wants children to look like little soldiers standing to attention. That is what has caused us to be stressed and anxious. Think back to the expression about somebody being 'up-tight'. No wonder. When people sit up like they have ramrods up their spines, breathing changes to the upper chest. Try it. They use the muscles that were given to us to highly-oxygenate the bloodstream so that we could fight off, or run away from, other predators in our cave days. They are part of our primeval heritage. If you look at animals other than Western humans you will notice that they always breathe lower down. They use the diaphragm rather than the muscles between the ribs. Those muscles are used for action, emergencies in particular. Watch a dog on a rug. All you see is the stomach moving. Say "walkies" and you will see that it primes itself by panting. It knows what to do because it has not been conditioned like its owners. Other animals know how to inflate their lungs, they are able to make their abdomens swell up with their breath when relaxing.'

I could see where this was going. He was going to ask me to get on all fours and pretend to be a dog. No way!

'I believe that we are like French dressing. The spirit is the vinegar and the body is the olive oil. Mix them together and you have life. Leave them and they divide. Breath is like the thing that keeps them together as an emulsion. When we die, there is no more breath and they separate. The spirit evaporates and we bury or burn the oil.

'Lay on your back, Gee'. He demanded. 'I will show you how to breathe properly.' He really wanted me to act like a dog!

Thankfully Miriam came back with the lads.

'What are you two doing?' she asked with a mixture of curiosity and amusement.

'I want him to lie on his back so I can teach him how to inflate himself properly.'

Miriam smiled. 'Yes he's finding that more difficult as he grows older. But what about the lessons in breathing that he told me you were going to teach him?'

Annan joined her joke by saying, 'I have explained that being stiff and upright are not always good things to be.' He was showing that he had a sharp sense of humour.

Miriam responded by smiling slightly and raising her right eyebrow into an arch. 'Come on boys, let's get some drinks.' She turned on her heel, looked at me with a frown and then strolled away. I would have felt less embarrassed if she had caught me with the topless girl from the day before. She had started the smut, after all.

Annan told me that we would continue and reeled off his commands. As instructed, I laid on my back, feet spread to about hip width, arms straight by my side. He placed two handfuls of sand on my stomach and told me to lift the sand up with my in-breath as if attempting to touch the sky. Then I had to hold my breath for a very slow count of four before lowering the sand 'as if trying to touch the backbone' for the same count. Then I had to leave it on my backbone for the same count before lifting it again.

'Four by four breathing, Gee. There are four moves each with a slow count of four. Simple, huh? Lift, hold, lower, leave.'

I wanted to humour Annan and at the same time see if there were any benefits from this public humiliation. I was aware that a small crowd had gathered, including our yawning neighbour and his wife. I closed my eyes to continue the cycle another five times.

To my surprise, I felt good. I was warm in my cheeks, I felt relaxed. Annan looked pleased and invited the members of our audience to participate. At this point they dissolved into the blue yonder muttering away in incomprehensible German and Italian. I wondered if they thought we were a gay couple doing our thing. I wanted Miriam to return to dispel that myth. As I said to Miriam later, 'Anyway, I am sure that had I been gay, somebody better looking than Annan would have accompanied me!'

'That is interesting. I feel really good. How does it work?' I thought that this would be useful for my clients, but I needed to know more. It seemed an alien way to breathe.

Annan looked happy. 'It is nothing more than breathing

as you were designed, and built, to do. You were using your diaphragm to breathe rather than your chest muscles. I told you that breathing is the key to life. Practice with a book at home if you want to avoid taking a big bag of sand with you.'

I sat up, dusted the sand from my stomach and lit a cigarette. I took in a deep drag of smoke.

'You are holding your cigarette with your right hand.' I knew Annan was going to lecture me about the harmful effects of smoking.

'Put your left hand on your stomach.'

I did.

'Now take a drag on your cigarette.'

As I did so, I noticed that my left hand moved outwards. I was using my diaphragm to inhale.

'The ironic thing about smoking, Gee, is that the only time a smoker breathes correctly is when they are smoking!'

'Bloody hell! That thought had never crossed my mind before. So what benefit is there in that piece of information?' I felt outsmarted by this man but also curious about how this had any relevance to me.

Annan was quiet for a while. 'Work it out for yourself. If I suggested to you that rather than being addicted to nicotine, the feeling described as withdrawal symptoms are really the negative effects of a build up of stale exhaust gases in the lower parts of your lungs, you would argue with me. The lungs are excretory organs. You need to flush the dirty air out. For however long you have been smoking, your cigarettes have been nothing more than a stimulus for you to breathe properly, or normally. The damage to your lungs and heart is a high price to pay for something that you should be doing naturally.'

He was silent for a while and then challenged me.

'Throw your cigarettes away in the bin when you leave the beach and consciously breathe with your diaphragm for the rest of the day. When you do that you will be free of what you thought were withdrawal symptoms. You will be a non-smoker. You will then be a little more willing to hear other secrets about yourself that will help you. But, before you throw them away, notice how similar the filter tips are to a weaning mother's nipple. The cigarette companies will stop at nothing to offer psychological reasons for people to smoke. I'll see you later.'

With that, Annan walked away.

I extinguished the cigarette in the sand and sat to ponder. I looked at the filter tip. I always thought it was a pattern that imitated cork from the early days of mass produced cigarettes. Why would any company go to the expense of printing the mouth end?

'Shit.' I said out loud.

'Is is safe to come back now? Have you finished making a spectacle of yourself?' The not so gentle tones of Miriam broke my trance.

'That man is interesting. He knows stuff. I think he has given me a way to stop smoking. I will give it a try.' My tone was serious enough to encourage Miriam sit down beside me.

'What do you mean?' She was more supportive now. She had known that I needed the holiday. I had been bad tempered and moody for a good number of weeks. She had noticed that my smoking had increased and she was keen for me to stop. Probably as much for the example I would set for the boys as for my own health.

'Coincidence, synchronicity, chance. All the great thinkers had a view about random meetings and events. Goethe, Jung and Einstein were all affected by it. I think that Annan is one of those people you meet who is a catalyst for change. In a way I guess my work is about change in my clients. Annan seems like somebody who will change the way I see the World. And all that happened is that we met on a flight.'

'Rather him than some blond bit.' Miriam's sarcasm had returned. 'So what are we going to do today? You promised the boys that we would go to the Water Park. We also want to visit Venice. Do you intend do spend more time with the Maharishi whatever-his-name-is?'

'Yes, I would like to, but you and the lads have priority. And please don't take the piss. He's after nothing apart from his own sense of doing-something-for-somebody-else. Maybe he gets a kick out of helping a therapist. Makes him feel superior, but I'm not so arrogant that I cannot accept help from anybody. I'm sure he has a lot more to say that will be useful for me.' I was beginning to feel irritated by Miriam's lack of enthusiasm.

In order to change the subject, I voiced some options for discussion. 'OK, let's visit Venice tomorrow, it's too late for today. And we'll go to the Water Park on Monday to avoid the weekend crowds.' I was decisive for once. As I waited for Miriam's agreement to my plans, the boys came running back.

She told them about our schedule and they agreed in perfect harmony in that wonderful way of youth in our current time. 'Whatever.'

We swam, played with a ball and sunbathed. I kept a discreet lookout for topless women as if they might endanger us if not detected. Miriam kept a watch on me. 'You are a dirty old man.' She muttered whilst watching a young Italian man walking through the edge of the water like a super-model on a catwalk. 'What's good for the goose is good for the gander.' She spat the words as she caught my eye witnessing her hypocrisy. 'At least he's not exposing himself like those young girls you watch.'

'No! That's not a pair of socks pushed down the front of his posing pouch, you know.' I returned as well as a Wimbledon champion.

I rolled over and closed my eyes. I thought that holidays were for repose rather than for point scoring. I desperately wanted a cigarette but concentrated on my breathing. The desire seemed to abate. When we left the beach to return to the caravan for lunch I threw my cigarettes into the bin as I had agreed.

Cheese, ham and bread washed down with water and followed with fresh and juicy peaches. When in Rome, etcetera.

After lunch, reminiscent of a school outing, we marched back to the beach for the afternoon in a crocodile file. It felt strange. Here we were, having escaped England, just sitting around doing nothing. It was the sun and the proximity of warm water that made it different. At home, during weekends, we would potter around in the garden or do odd jobs around the house. Here, we were content not doing anything, not that there was a garden to tend nor a house that needed repair.

The luxury of being a hunter-gatherer in years-gone-by was that there was always time to relax and chat with your fellows after the prey was caught. In our lives now, hunting and gathering took just moments in the supermarket, so time to spent garnering fees from clients was available. That means that we never have enough time to sit to relax and chat with friends and family, unless we are on holiday.

Late in the afternoon we wandered back to our temporary home like a band of travellers with the towels, balls, sunshades, Frisbee and empty water bottles. I volunteered to go to the shop to buy meat, vegetables, bread, wine and water for supper.

When I returned the boys were sitting in the loungers. Both were wearing earphones and were nodding to music. They looked like deaf old people in a home shuddering at their memories.

There was a bicycle that looked as if it had been thrown onto the ground in front of the awning. Miriam was sitting at the table drinking a glass of wine with a vicar. 'Godfrey, this is the Reverend...sorry, but I missed your name!'

'Walter Evans.' The vicar reached out his hand without getting up. He looked like Friar Tuck. I wondered if he was the musician who had another role in the camp. His voice was everything that was expected from a vicar. A slight lisp, good middle class diction and a timbre of all-knowingness. 'I'm here suffering for God.' he joked, tucking his Polo shirt into his shorts. 'Every two years I get sent out here for a few weeks to give services in the camp church. It's terrible, all the good food and wine. Nobody has any problems here. If somebody dies they get flown home. A few pop into the church on a Sunday and that's it. Yes, that's what I call suffering.' He broke into a laugh that confirmed that he really was Robin Hood's monk.

We talked while we witnessed Walter drinking most of a bottle of our wine. Miriam was happy and chatted to him about what he did when he was in England.

It transpired that he was a prison chaplain so I guess he needed his time away as much as I did. Listening to the guilt and remorse of prisoners who must have included wife beaters, rapists and child molesters would have been difficult. We were similar in so-much-as we both had to give unconditional positive regard to people we would ordinarily be judgmental about. However, he dealt with the perpetrators and I was involved with their victims. My sense of satisfaction in releasing people from their nightmares must be greater than his as he offered the promise of Divine pardon. Perhaps not. There must be a lot of gratification in being an agent of God with the power of forgiveness for the unforgivable.

'Before you go,' my hint was fairly obvious but I was hungry, 'what is the Holy Spirit? I know who God is supposed to be and I know who Jesus is but I've no idea what the Holy Ghost is meant to be.' I had asked this question of a number of churchmen but they never gave a straight answer. I know that I was being provocative but maybe it was left over from Annan's lecture on breathing holding the spirit of life to the body.

'I must be off in a minute. Let me think about it and I'll come back to you tomorrow.'

'We're in Venice tomorrow so perhaps Friday.' I asserted.

'I'll do that if you promise to come to my service on Sunday.' The vicar was equally forceful.

Blackmail from a vicar! Conditional terms, I thought.

'We'd love to.' Miriam answered for me.

'Good. See you Friday'. Walter left with a cheery laugh. He picked up his bike and wobbled away down the road.

I turned to my bag of shopping warming nicely in the bag in the evening sunset.

As I unpacked the food Miriam told me that Annan had stopped by. She said that they had chatted about breathing and he had asked her to encourage me to remain a non smoker. Until then I had given little thought to cigarettes and felt proud of myself. She had talked to him about my weight and the possibility that I might put on more pounds after stopping smoking. He told her that he would pop by later to have a word with me.

At that moment he appeared, smiling broadly and sat

down without invitation. The boys went back to their music.

'So, you're worried about putting on weight. I'll help you on Friday if that's all right with you. I understand that you are in Venice tomorrow.'

'Will you help me as well?' Miriam's vanity had got the better of her. She disliked wearing a bikini on the beach, protesting that a one piece costume was more fitting for a woman of her age and shape.

'Of course.' Annan missed the opportunity to flatter her by reassuring her that her figure was fine as it was. 'I'll see you both at ten o'clock on the beach on Friday. Same place as today.

He started to walk away but beckoned me to him. In a confidential tone he said 'Tomorrow, take the boat to the island of Torcello on your way into Venice. You can either go via the islands or directly to the city. On Torcello, go to the Cathedral, Santa Maria dell'Assunta. Look at the mosaic floor. If you have ever seen those Magic Eye pictures, look at the floor in the same way. De-focus your eyes, stare at the floor and you will receive an important religious message. Take a photograph of it if you can. We'll talk about it on Friday.

We heard instruments being tuned and some opera singers going through their scales. We were being reminded that there was to be some entertainment in the square that evening.

After our dinner, cooked this time by Miriam, we made our way through the hedge and arrived, like supporting singers, at the front. We hid in the shadows as all the chairs had occupants.

The concert started with a tenor going through a piece by Mozart. It went on far too long. He was replaced by a lavish soprano who was better to look at than to hear. Miriam caught my expression. 'You have the temperament of a vulture. You wait, dribble and try to consume.'

All I could say was 'I am a man. That is my nature. You wait to see what will happen if the next act is Andreas Bocelli.'

It was not. Instead it was a rotund little man whose talents were firmly based on dramatics. We smiled as he foppishly pranced around the stage. That was the highlight of the evening. After he took his applause we decided to return to the comfort of our little haven outside the caravan and listen to the remainder of the concert at a distance.

Perhaps it was the holiday spirit or the vicar's religious spirit earlier, maybe the melodies, but yet again, I drank far too much red wine that evening. As the music took on an ecclesiastical lilt, my mind wondered what I would find in the mosaic. Was the message put there by the masons or was it added by a higher authority? Was it created in the process of building or did it appear afterwards as if by magic? We all love finding the answers to mysteries.

However, the Chianti pulled my thoughts to order as a dog is drawn to heel and it told me to lie down and go to sleep.

CHAPTER FOUR

HOLY VISIONS

thursday

Some of the aliens were hostile. The huge grey ones would stand on the sky and would spear the fish from time to time. That was horrible, and caused panic. Black monsters in suits of armour attacked the baby fish, sometimes. But there seemed to be a God. Now and again the fish would seem to see his face smiling from above the sky. He dropped food onto the sky. They would swim up to eat it. The religious fish called this 'Matter from Heaven.'

It was on that day that I came to understand that there are two Gods.

On the island of Torcello we went into the cathedral recommended by Annan. I found the mosaic floor. It was beautiful in the golden light that was streaming through the window that lit it in a fittingly divine way.

I stared, as instructed, but was unable to see through the pattern to the cryptic message hidden within. I moved around to look at it from differing angles. There was nothing that leapt at me. I gazed for minutes, defocusing my eyes, squinting through my half closed eyelids then opening them wide. The message was not to be seen. After a while I became aware of a uniformed man hovering near me like a store detective after a shop-lifter.

I took out my camera and moved into a position whereby I could capture as much of the floor as possible. Immediately I was harried out of the way by the official. I understand hardly any Italian but the message was clear. Photography was forbidden. Even in the days of cameras that will adjust to the light conditions to avoid flashlight, it was prohibited. I was pushed in the direction of a sign, written in various languages, telling everybody so. The miserable man then pointed me towards a stand where I could buy postcards. Here was the rub. I became convinced that photography was banned in order to gain extra revenue. I had paid an admission fee for four of us, so how much profit was expected?

Even so, I bought some cards because I wanted to study the mosaics. If I was unable to look at them or take my own pictures, then a postcard would have to do. I wondered if the picture would have been had been doctored to hide the message. My mood became grumpy. My hangover did not help.

The next boat was due to leave in thirty minutes and so we paid yet more money to climb the tower. The stairway was steep and I was breathless by the time we reached the top. Even though the views were wonderful, my major concern was the way I felt. I was sweating, my heart pounded. I wondered if I had strained my heart to its bursting point. All I wanted to do was to return to ground level.

Despite my fears I ran down the stairs and emerged into little square where tourist mementoes are sold. I bought some water, drank it and waited for the rest of my family to join me. The small village was the home of vendors. There were a few fishing boats lying on the grass by the water, but the inhabitants made their livings from passing trade. It was as if the church was the song of the sirens drawing visitors to the shores to spend money. The church was the main attraction and it wanted to make the most money.

After I reassured Miriam that I was going to live, we waited at the dock.

We travelled on to Venice on the little ferryboat via the other islands. I looked at the postcard pictures hoping to find a secret message. "The meaning of life is..."

Alas, I could find nothing. I wondered if any code from the craftsmen of old would be in Latin or in old Italian. I struggled with the idea that church builders held so much mysterious information that they fabricated it into architecture for future generations to find. Did they really put the prime secret into a conundrum more difficult to solve than a Rubik's Cube? And if they knew the answers, why did they not share them rather than encrypt them? Freemasonry is full of secrets never to be shared and that seem to date back to the Holy Grail. What power could that hold? I wondered if this was a false idol that should not be revered.

Perhaps it was merely a symbol of intimidating power.

However hard I stared at the pictures I was still unable to find any hidden truths other than the obvious one that I had paid for something that I should have had a right to copy myself.

The holy commercialisation was repeated throughout the day. Every church charged its entrance fee and then wanted more money for 'add-ons'. Almost like a sleazy masseuse. 'Anything extra, sir?'

The business places had a different approach. Get the punters into the glass-blowing factories for a demonstration and sell them product. Elsewhere, the artists performed with their oils and acrylics and then offered their wares. At least there was no pressure. We could watch for the entertainment and then walk away for free. The contrast was tremendous between those creators of beauty who would sell it, and the jailers of ancient art who wanted to be given money to look at it. Those artworks belonged to the church, that hugely rich chain of the supernatural men, alleging more influence with God the higher they stood. Would a bishop or cardinal have to pay to look at the treasures? Almost certainly not. It would be their right. After all, they worked for the company that owned them.

Again, my mind played with the thought of the mediaeval masons who might have played power games with the church leaders by hiding cryptic messages in their work. Perhaps they really did know spiritual secrets that they did not want to share with their religious paymasters. They must have worked with churchmen often enough to see duplicity.

We watched and listened to a classical guitar player in a small square in Venice. His smile that captivated Miriam and his brilliance as a musician were free. No promises of immortality if we bought his CDs, but the memory of the experience sufficed. We did buy a CD, however, but from choice rather than coercion.

Thankfully I was not wearing shorts when we entered San Marco Cathedral. My full length trousers covered my not so full length legs. However, Miriam had to cover her shoulders out of respect for something that was not explained. I found it strange that we had to cover ourselves up in order to see paintings and statues of Jesus and Mary in various states of undress. There was Jesus wearing nothing more than a loin cloth and Mary baring her breasts in paintings. I could not work out the incongruity. It was a show of power by holy men over ordinary folk.

Venice is a place that is unequalled in its charm, but the corporation of the church is the owner. Strange, when the history of the city is stained with the blood of so many people killed in the name of God!

My mood was not only caused by my spiritual confrontation, but more by the lack of faith in my heart that I experienced at the top of the cathedral tower on Torcello.

At least the route to the top of the Campanile in Venice was by an elevator. As I looked over the Piazza San Marco, once again my heart raced, I felt dizzy and I thought that I was going to die. I had to escape by pushing my way through the queue of people waiting for the lift. My manner and complexion avoided too many negative reactions. Once I had reached ground level my breathing calmed down and I gained some sort of composure.

Miriam appeared to be concerned when she eventually joined me with the boys.

'I thought I was having a heart attack. I felt awful.' I dribbled out. I was used to the symptoms of anxiety and panic from my work, but this was the second time in one day that I had first-hand experience. After a litre of water I returned to a shaky version of my normal self in time for dinner in one of the many restaurants that adorned the waterfront. I ate very little. My appetite was crushed when I witnessed the chef fondling the buttocks of one of the young male waiters. I was sure he would not have washed his hands before handling my salad.

After finding our way through the narrow alleys and climbing over a multitude of bridges we got back to St Mark's square.

We caught a late ferry back to the mainland. As we chugged along, Annan's words on the plane came to my mind. 'Men have become jealous of the creative power of God, and they want to destroy His masterpiece'.

This was the creator who allowed men to take the reins

by giving us language, conscious thought, opposing thumbs and conflicting minds. He gave the human apes the keys to the palace and we have ripped the shiny things of beauty off the planet as monkeys still do to cars in safari parks.

My notepad became the recipient of my bile.

"Men wanted, and still desire, power and they usurped the essence of that creator by inventing a human God who ruled the planet with anger and pain. Those shamanic cultures of fifty thousand years ago that involved medicine men and healers were mutated into a superstition of eternal corporal punishment. Do as I say, or rather as my concocted God says, or you will be punished. Hey, don't blame me. I am the messenger, the go-between. However, do as I say. Pay your dues. Treat me as a substitute for the Spirit of Life. Bow down to me. The arbiters were the traders in hope. In return for food, money and power they could intervene to guarantee a place in Heaven. They built a sales team of priests and missionaries whose job it was to get more customers with a hard sell. If they could not get a foot in the door, they broke it down with force. As sales grew, they appointed team leaders who in turn became regional managers under the denominational directors reporting into the CEO.

"God, the unseen chairman, was portrayed as the Supreme Being who made policy and who initiated disciplinary action for the non believers but whose authority was misappropriated. Even the boss's son was inducted into the business. He upset some of the directors and was dealt with brutally for attempting to bring love and compassion into play for the customers. After he was cruelly removed by being nailed to a cross, the competition was fiercely fought and eradicated in his name. Witches and critics were burnt at the stake. Wars of acquisition were fought in the name of the business, the promise of afterlife being the bonus for being killed; the whitener in the soapsuds. Even the Protestant Church of England had been an attempt at a management buy-out that resulted in a competitor being formed. Generic brands were created."

I came out of my introspection, blurting to Miriam in such a way that I was pleased that most people on the boat within earshot were not native English speakers. 'Do you think that if Jesus came back today, he'd be a Christian? I don't think so. He threw the money traders out of the temples. He didn't employ them to raise funds to expand a dogma by selling views of artworks. If we owned a masterpiece, would we charge our friends to look at it? The money is not for security, God protects the church. Anyway, why do churches have lightning conductors on their spires?' I looked at Miriam.

She looked back at me as if I had gone mad. 'And all that because they wanted to charge you fifty cents for a postcard? You'll rot in Hell, I reckon'. Miriam wanted her final word on the subject, but I continued.

'I think that Jesus was a great shaman who wanted men to recognise God the Spirit. I think that Mohammed was the same. Yet greed and the lust for the ultimate power, the ability to kill fellow men and other creatures for gain or pleasure, grew large again. The Holy Wars, the crusades were part of that. I can understand the current wrath of Islam at being condemned by the Western Christian world because they own oil. It is easier to breed hatred for a religion than to admit that the West wants to exploit the resources of other lands. Perhaps the conflicts are the Universe's attempt to restrict the burning of oil to slow global warming and the further raping of our Mother Earth. While people in Florida worry about the state of the world, they keep cool by burning oil to feed their air-conditioning units. Who cares anymore?'

'For Christ's sake, shut up, Gee. You sound like a babbling fool. Not only do you sound like one, I think you have convinced me that you are one.' Miriam, at last, had the final word.

The ferry trip back became uncomfortable. I felt sick but managed to retain the meagre contents of my stomach for the duration of the journey. Once back at the caravan, however, I felt the need to rush to the toilet block.

'Oh God!' I vomited. The strings of regurgitated pasta and tomato sauce were like worms covered in blood. They looked like monsters staring back at me in shock that I had eaten them. The thought made me retch even more. I despatched more of them to their watery graves.

'Oh God!' I repeated as if He would do something about it. No answer. I gagged again.

In times of crisis, we pray. At other times we become self sufficient. God must have His busiest time at the end of parties and when the bars close. Perhaps we need to be conditioned to say the word at the end of our lives so that we say the Almighty's name with our final breath. Or does it become a blasphemous expletive that blames somebody else for our extinction?

Anyway, I had not been drunk. I had only consumed two glasses of wine with my dinner. It was something to do with the panic attack I had in Venice. After washing my face I walked back to our temporary home, crawled into bed and fell asleep to the sounds of Miriam laughing with the boys in the awning. She sought the safety of sane companions. I worried that all my strange thoughts would come back to me as a nightmare.

CHAPTER FIVE

LIFTING MY SPIRITS

friday

A lot of time was spent in intellectual debate on the meaning of life and whether God really did exist or not. Even though he appeared on a regular basis, he did not seem to do much to give a quality of life to the fish, apart from dropping bits of food into the pond that supplemented their diet.

'How are you this morning?' Miriam's face appeared over the top of a cup of coffee.

'Like shit! Must have been something that I ate yesterday.' My voice was a growl escaping through phlegm.

'Your guru awaits you outside' I was informed.

'We said we would meet him at ten.' I protested.

'It is eleven o'clock already.' Miriam informed me.

Tell him to go away, please. I'm in no mood for his bullshit. Tell him I'll meet him on the beach after lunch.' My mood was not improving with the induction of caffeine.

'We're going to the beach now. Are you coming or staying?'

My answer was given by putting down my cup, rolling over and closing my eyes.

'See you later then. Is there anything that you need?'

'Just some peace and quiet'.

I fell asleep.

When I awoke, I stirred and sat outside on one of the loungers. A short while later I watched Miriam and the boys coming back.

'You know, I have to apologise. Annan is not what I thought. He talked to me about controlling my weight, or rather my shape. It makes sense.' Miriam's enthusiasm was refreshing.

'He explained that fat is wonderful stuff. It is part of our survival systems that have kept us going against all odds for hundreds of thousands of years. Back then, there were no refrigerators, deep freezers. There were no shops, so the only place a mother could store food hygienically was in her body as fat.

'Enough!' I requested. 'Tell me later please. My stomach is still a bit queasy. Talking about fat is making it worse.'

'So do you want any lunch? She asked.

'Not at the moment. I'll have a glass of wine, though.'

Miriam frowned as she was setting out some bread, cold meats and cheese. 'Have fruit juice instead.'

I drank two glasses of wine.

We wandered back to the beach in the afternoon. Annan was sitting in what had become our usual spot. Miriam greeted him and then walked to the edge of the sea with the lads as if pre-arranged. My heart sank.

'Hi, Gee. Are you better now? Miriam said you weren't too well yesterday. You had a panic or something.'

I knew I was in for some more advice from this man. 'Who the hell is he, anyway? He's a bloody know-it-all, that's for sure.' I thought.

'Have you been doing your breathing?' The interrogative tone set my nerves on edge.

'No. I didn't feel well yesterday. I think it's because I stopped smoking. I bought a pack this morning and had a couple. Please don't tell Miriam. She's in a bad mood with me as it is.' I was talking in that confidential whisper that my clients sometimes use when telling something about their guilty thoughts.

'And do you feel better for them?' His tone was like the spoof I use when discussing counsellors who get stuck on a series of 'And how did that make you feel?' with their first finger touching the point of the chin.

'Better.' I was going to be truthful.

'That's because you changed your breathing with the cigarette as I explained to you. You forgot to breathe properly and you craved for clean air in your lungs rather than for nicotine. That's what happened when you had your panic attack, I bet. Your breathing became high and rapid. You were supercharging your system to fight off, or escape from, a threat that was unreal. You hyperventilated and went into a panic because there was no subsequent, intense release. You had nothing to fight with and nowhere to run.

You were like a car at traffic lights with your foot hard on the accelerator.' The lecture had begun.

'So. Can you help me?' I omitted the smart-arse.

'Yes, but you have to want me to help you, however. You seem to be uncooperative and a little hostile. But you, as a therapist, have encountered that many times with your clients. Trust me, Gee. You have many problems that must be addressed. Open your mind, lower your defences and let me give you a physical and mental...what do they call it on the television...make-over?' He laughed.

I took his point. Here I was on holiday with a wife who I was falling out with, two sons who I had virtually ignored, smoking and drinking too much, overweight and highly stressed. I considered that I had little to lose except my problems. I should have known how to deal with them. I should have kept up my meetings with my supervisor. I wondered if I was burning out. I spent my working life listening to, and attempting to resolve, problems for others. That had a negative effect on my mind. That much I knew. Physician, heal thyself.

'So how much are you going to charge me?' I guess I was, once again, stereotyping this well-off Indian. I assumed he was a trader who sold solutions for money.

Annan looked shocked. He leant across and firmly spoke in a low, but firm, tone. 'Screw you, Gee. You asked me that before. Sharing something is different to selling. The problem with our modern way of life is that even though we have plenty, we are unable to share. That is why people starve to death in Africa while obese Westerners watch them on television with a TV supper on their laps. Sure they can feel sorry, but more likely they become happy that they are not in that sort of mess. Lesson one is to understand the intentions of others. Some of us want to give rather than gain.'

I was stuck for words. I was embarrassed. He had read the sarcastic tone of my question and responded accordingly. It was the slap that I needed.

'I am so sorry. That is why I should seek help, I guess. I have lost the plot a bit. Sorry, Annan.'

Annan looked straight into my eyes, searching for any

remnants of soul that I might have. 'Breath, as I told you, is the essence of life. It is what we think of as God. Breath is what flows through the Universe. Not breathing as in a puff of wind, but as in inspiration. We borrow life from the Universe, we never own it. Mosquitoes thrive in stagnant water. Without breath or clean air, undesirable things breed in us.'

He was quiet for about a minute as if he had been transported to a private place and then he looked at me with a smile and said, 'OK. Let's get started. Did you do as I asked on the island?'

'I looked at the mosaics yesterday as you told me to do. I couldn't see anything and I wasn't allowed to take photographs. I had to buy some postcards. I looked at them but couldn't see anything.' I wanted to show that I had followed his advice in some way.

'Tell me what you see after you have studied them very well, again.' Annan had donned the manner of a teacher. I waited for the word 'grasshopper' to end his comment.

'I thought a lot about religion. I think that God has been taken hostage by the church or that He is sleeping.' With that comment, as if being admonished by the Almighty, I was smacked in the face by a beach ball. As I was about to shout, the thunder started. The wind drove clouds of sand up the beach and people were dismantling umbrellas and collecting towels.

Miriam called to the boys. 'Back to the caravan. A storm is breaking.'

Annan and I watched the sand being whipped up by the ever strengthening gusts, stinging our eyes and any exposed flesh. The sky grew dark and the rain started. We moved swiftly to avoid getting too wet. By the time we got back to the house on wheels we were soaking and out of breath.

The storm turned into a deluge and the rumbles of thunder became powerful explosions as they drew closer.

Sitting under the awning and talking about God in a thunderstorm was a surreal experience. The conversation was illuminated by lightning and then punctuated by the sound of heavy rain on the canvass and the low growling of thunder as it moved away.

Referring to my notepad, I told Annan about my thoughts on the ferry. I explained that I felt cheated by being forbidden to photograph what should have been in the public domain, and for being charged for looking at works of art.

Smiling as a flash of lightning scorched the air above us, he commented, 'There is no need for you to look for the mosaic's message anymore. You found it.'

I felt puzzled. I had seen nothing in the thousands of little coloured stones.

The thunder rolled as I prepared to query his words. He continued before my words came out. 'Religion is a business. It is a corporation. You find that the higher up the corporate ladder the employees go, the less spiritual they seem to become. Knowledge is power and the more knowledge that people have that others lack, then the more power can be wielded. Secret knowledge is part of ritual. Ritual is what stops ordinary folk from being able to be spiritual. Their religions impose rules that have to be obeyed in order to appreciate life after they have died. I have always been intrigued by the modern Hollywood image of witchcraft. Like prayers and responses, spells need to be learnt and they must be delivered in special, esoteric ways. It is a strange thing that the supernatural entities only seem to hear in Latin yet the demons haunt, hate and curse in the everyday language of their victims.'

The lightning flashed again. I shuddered when the thunder detonated above.

'You see. If the scene is set correctly, more power is added. If I had been a religious man searching for the souls of other men, I would have studied the weather and delivered my proclamations against a backdrop of a day like today. Wind and rain, hail and loud noises. I would have predicted eclipses and sold them as signs from the Heavens. Yet, the seers of old knew the weather patterns. Power was, and is, knowledge. And power is the lifeblood of the corporation.'

My attention was fixed on Annan's words for the first time. I was hungry for more. 'So, when you say the holy men look for the souls of others, what do you mean?'

He rolled on. 'The corporations, whether the church,

business or governments only want to sell the brand. The individual has no room in a company. The individual is the person who has a soul. The soul is not the thing that devils want to steal but it is a belief in life and happiness and the world on which we live. If we care too much for those things then we might protest against the felling of rain forests to make flat-pack furniture. We might buy smaller cars that use less gasoline. We might feel happy with the land we have rather than using force to invade other countries. We might just become the human that we feel inside but seem impelled to deny. We work for money rather than food. Money is the symbol of power. That is why I refused payment for helping you. I want you to recover your soul, Gee. Your soul is part of the God of Spirituality. The God image used by religion is the thing that takes away the souls of men. They are mortgaged for the promise of a reward after our bodies and minds have worn out in the production of wealth for corporations.'

I was beginning to see the God that I intuitively knew was the real one.

Annan, continued. 'Did God create man in his own image or did man create God as a man who lives in the sky to ensure that we looked up in our spiritual moments to avoid looking at the real creation, our planet? Was it to prevent us from seeing God in ourselves and every living thing? God is not a man. God is the essence and the energy of all things above, below and around us. We are connected, as every point of a spider's web was at some point connected, to the builder's body. And everything is still connected to the whole. Shamans and the older witches knew that. That is why they have been eradicated or subdued. Their truth conflicts with the man made imagery of a super-power. That creation of God in a man's image stops us looking at the magnificent planet on which we live. While men are looking for God in the sky, their eyes are diverted from seeing the theft from, and the raping of, the organ and spirit of our creation, our Mother Earth.

'We are individuals in our primeval roots. We are also pack animals that will follow leaders for safety, order and security. When we became big societies we had to be controlled by the powers of force by using soldiers. The leaders became monsters instead of alpha males. They had the strength of force to murder others. They could invent mating ceremonials in order to rape. It is said that big is beautiful. Big is ugly. Small is better. With small, the leaders are able to be challenged. They are accountable. Corporations are beyond reach. You have no say in the tax rates levied on you. You have no influence over the prices pharmaceutical companies charge for their drugs. Above all, you lack the right to refuse. The President is not chosen by the American people, he is chosen by fellow politicians and businessmen. The voters only vote for one man. The same applies to the Prime Minister of Britain. There is no choice, only an apparition of democracy. And if either of them does things that upsets the population, like starting the Iraq War, how the hell do you get rid of them? You can't.'

I was now listening and processing at a pace. I nodded to Annan to carry on.

'By the way, the word Parliament comes from the root word that means 'speaking'. Where is the part in the mother of democracy that refers to 'listening'? And the very word "corporation" comes from the root for a body made of flesh. Souls are emotional. When souls are claimed then it is easier to get people to sacrifice their flesh in wars. The promise is that when the body is lost, the soul is saved and lives on. That pledge of immortality goes to the heart of emotional blackmail.

'I run a benevolent company. One that gives far more than it takes. My corporate goal is to ease suffering by protecting the innocent at the expense of the guilty.

'I remember in a village in India, the people would chase the monkeys away in case they tried to steal food. One day I saw a monkey with a broken arm wandering down the road. I asked why it had not been killed or chased away. I was told that as it was unable to look after itself, then it became the responsibility of the villagers to care for it. In that simple way, a whole new philosophy of life emerged for me.'

The storm had moved on to make holiday makers further up the coast swarm back to their shelters.

Annan got up and prepared to go. 'I've said enough. I'll

see you tomorrow morning. If you want, we'll get to grips with the panic.'

'No. We'll just chill out tomorrow.' I asserted. I felt that we should spend some time as a family. We needed to start to enjoy our holiday.

He shouted his farewells to Miriam and the lads in the caravan. Miriam came out to plant a small kiss on his cheek.

With the perfect timing of an amateur theatrical group's play, as Annan left, Walter arrived on his bicycle. Two opposing sides adding contrast to my bewildered mind.

'God works in mysterious ways.' He said, pointing to the sky. A cliché to start the conversation. A well worked line, I thought.

'I was going to bring a bottle of wine' he hinted. 'But the storm made life a bit difficult. Riding a metal horse in a thunderstorm needs a huge act of faith.'

'I'll open a bottle. Hold on.' I went inside, winked at Miriam and told her, 'Walter of the altar has descended upon us. His halo got a bit wet and he needs a bottle of red to dry it out.'

'Evans-above is how I think of him.' Miriam was smiling more than she had for weeks. 'I was listening to what Annan was saying and although I might disagree with parts, I think he has a point. I'll join you with the vicar. We'll see what he has to say. I'll bring the plonk.'

Walter was looking smug. 'I was thinking about your question.' He pulled out a piece of paper. 'As non-theological answers, the Holy Spirit is like the fizz in Coca Cola. It is the producer of true personality and character. If you like, it is God's therapy for nerdy people. Look, I've written that down for you so that you can think about it.' Walter handed me a small Gideon's Bible. He put the paper inside the cover. I pulled it out. It was a timetable for church services. 'Will I see you on Sunday?'

'Yes, of course.' Miriam answered for us both, again.

As if to exact another price for our attendance, she looked at Walter and asked 'So what is the soul in theological terms? How do we lose it? Who takes it? What do they do with it?'

'Hold on.' Walter almost screamed. One question at a

time, or better still don't ask. The soul is what we have as humans that the animals miss. It is what makes us human.'

Miriam was feeling provocative. 'But what humans have is the ability to kill for pleasure. And to rape and torture. Other animals don't do that. Is that what a soul does for you? Is that what makes us human?'

Walter refused the bait. He looked at his watch, got up and said 'See you Sunday' as his goodbye. He even left half a glass of wine. Miriam and I laughed as he rushed away on his chariot of ire.

'Are we becoming obsessed with religion?' I asked Miriam.

'I don't know. You once said that you were the biggest atheist that God had created. That was when we had first met. Can an atheist be born again? I hope not. There is nothing more zealous than a convert.' Miriam smiled.

With a grin I replied. 'That was a joke. It is like the lines I have heard since from clients. Great quotes such as "she was terminally ill when she died" and "she is bilingual in six languages" are wonderful' I quipped.

She looked at me in that soft way that she had seduced me with twenty years before. 'Shall we make love tonight? It has been over a week now and we are on holiday in romantic Italy. The boys won't hear anything under their headphones.' She chuckled in a way that would turn the stone heart of a statue to flesh but make the flesh of a man turn as hard as stone.

And so it came to pass.

We gave the boys some money, encouraged them to explore the site and crept into the caravan. When they returned, they wondered why their mother and father were giggling so much.

'How much wine have you two drunk since we went out?' asked Mark with the look of disapproval parents should give to sons when caught with their girlfriends in compromising situations. That made us giggle even more.

Later, after we had all settled down, Miriam and I cuddled each other as we had not for a long time.

The first flash of lightning was followed by a loud explosion. 'Oh, shit! We're in a metal can. God is after me again.' I grumbled as I rolled over and fell asleep.

CHAPTER SIX

WANDERING STARS

saturday

The fish wondered what life was like outside their world. They tried to talk to the frogs, but they could not establish a language for communication. The frogs would either be mating or hiding. They didn't really seem to belong there. And, the Great Diving Beetles were too repulsive to want to get to know. There were newts from time to time that would arrive to gobble up all sorts of food from fish eggs to bits of mud. Or so it seemed. They were no great company, either.

'Let's go shopping today.' Miriam had this way of offering a suggestion that was really an instruction. If I refused then I would be assigned the responsibility of entertaining everybody for the day. Miriam liked shopping for clothes whereas I enjoyed buying food. The two were very often incompatible.

The boys had the great idea of going to the beach, which was beginning to lose its appeal for me. Too much of the same. At their ages, the need to worry about their welfare had just about gone. So Miriam packed the beach bags for the lads and we made our way past the security guards to get a bus. I could not resist pretending to hide my face under the peak of my baseball cap as we showed our passes.

We hit the town in a different mood. Our romantic evening had changed us into two young lovers who would hold hands and sneak a little cuddle here and there.

We came across a market in the middle of the town. We saw fish for sale that had been swimming just a few hours earlier. We saw fruits and vegetables that had earth and blemishes on them. There were imperfectly shaped tomatoes that we could smell before we saw them. All of this was the produce of small farmers and little fishing boats that painted a scene that was a million miles from the mass produced supermarket fare that we were used to at home.

Miriam bought some shorts and two blouses. She also bought a sweat shirt each for the lads as if she needed to bring gifts back for not having them dragging behind us in that way that they could adopt all too easily.

We stopped for lunch at a café that had an outdoor area. Our choices were not surprising. It was a case of deciding which pizza topping would we have. We ordered a bottle of red wine, which we started straight away.

'Do you think we are drinking too much, Gee?' Miriam smiled.

"Not yet. Hey, we're on holiday.'

After two glasses each, the pizzas arrived. Tomato, anchovy and cheese for Miriam, tomato, anchovy, cheese and artichoke hearts for me. Such are the joys of life!

'What is this religious quest that you are on?' Miriam asked in a way that was both sarcastic and curious.

I answered as truthfully as I was able. 'I don't know. It is like an obsession, but it is also a coincidence. This guy Annan seems to be fuelling something that had been sitting there dormant. I guess it was something that was said on the flight out here. He said something about civilisation and its connection to modern religion. It went on from there. Unlike women, men seem to be unable to remember conversations verbatim, so the detail has become lost.'

'What you are saying is that women have better memories than men.' Miriam smiled and added, 'do you think it has anything to do with your work? You have been very busy, lately and I worry about your health.'

'My mental health, perhaps. No I'm not burning out.' That was one of the worries that therapists have. That is why we have supporters, usually called supervisors.

More wine was poured and another bottle ordered.

I continued. 'No. I think it's just that my mind wants a chase and the quarry was chosen by serendipity. It is something I have thought about, on and off, for a long time. Clients talk about dead relatives. Often they seek answers from sources that are on the fringe. Mediums and spiritual guides of all types including vicars and priests. When the answers are given, they are usually vague enough to allow the listener to find what they want. Jung called it subjective interpretation.'

I let out a sigh, and continued. 'People want real answers and there are very few. How can I tell people that it is about biology and luck when all they want to know is that it will get better? How can you explain to somebody that their father abused them because he was an unfeeling and uncaring pervert? God, as we know Him, does not provide solutions. People pray but do not receive a response. That is what makes Annan interesting. He has inspired me to think that perhaps we are asking questions in the wrong direction. Nietzsche said, "God is dead." Perhaps he meant that the God created by man never existed but the spirit of life in men, other animals, the plants and every other thing on the planet has been denied in modern life. We should look elsewhere for God. The spirit of life is staring at us but we are blind to its presence.'

Miriam attempted to pull me out of the quicksand that I was about to enter. 'Don't most people use God as an insurance company? Pay in the prayers and when damage has been done, call on God to settle the claim. You offer the same sort of hope to your clients. Shit happens to them and you do your best to salvage whatever good you can from their pasts. Then you rebuild it so that they can face whatever might happen in their futures. You deal with the effects of man's inhumanity to man a lot of the time. That is not God's responsibility to fix, it is ours, as a species and as a culture to prevent things going wrong in the first place.'

'Precisely,' I answered and then I was silent for a while.

'Why aren't mediums called media in the plural?' Miriam had to add with a smile. 'Come on, leave your office and play in the sunshine for a few days.' She poured some more wine for both of us.

'Coincidence always fascinates me.' Miriam almost seemed to be changing the subject. 'This chap, Annan. What do you know about him? One day you meet him on a 'plane, then he turns up at our camp. After that he appears to have enough time to spend helping you to stop smoking. Is he a Saint, a do-gooder, a lonely old fool or just a nuisance?'

I had no answers. Annan had been as slippery as an eel whenever I had tried to find out more about him. He would always turn enquiries back at me.

'What did he do to help you to lose weight?' I thought I might find some answers about this man from Miriam.

'Well, we have agreed to talk in more detail early next week. What he said is what I have already told you. It is to do with changing my body-shape blueprint, whatever that is. I'll tell you more when I know more. Shall we order some more vino?' Miriam was getting a little drunk.

We resisted the call for more alcohol and, laden with shopping, we made our way back to the invulnerable Caravan Park where we found the lads sheltering from the sun under the awning.

They had not eaten and were waiting for their parents to bring food, like chicks sitting in a nest anticipating beak-loads of grubs. In our drink inspired mood, we cooked some pasta for them. It was the closest thing to worms we could find.

We spent the late afternoon on the beach but were sensible enough not to swim.

After our meal in the evening, cooked using the fresh markets foodstuffs that we had bought, we became aware of another act warming up in the square.

'Shall we go?' I asked.

Miriam's 'yes' was matched by the lads' refusal. 'We'll explore the camp site tonight.' They wanted to drink beer and meet some girls, I suspected.

Miriam and I poured some wine into plastic beakers and then walked through the hole in the hedge. We found some seats and waited for the Country 'n Western artist to appear.

A middle aged man in a big Stetson walked onto the stage with his guitar. His moustache made him look like a walrus. His old leather jacket had "www.crokum.com" emblazoned on it in silver studs. Then he sang. It was awful. He was a spoof of talent. His songs were based on the immortal ideas that 'babies dun leave you' and 'dogs have dun died'.

Dwayne Crokum was a phoney, it was so apparent. Sadly the joke did not work on an audience whose native tongues did not allow the humour to come across.

Between his songs he had a patter that tried to tie them

together as a comical autobiography. In this way, he bulked up his act with silly dialogue. 'Ah faked ma own death. Ah pretended that I was shot on stage to build ma record sales.' He said in a long Southern drawl. 'Ma obituary said that I was the worst artist that ever hit Nashville, but they was glad that Nashville hit me back.' That story, as with all the others, was met with stony silence.

Dwayne was not happy. 'Screw you all. If you can't recognise a celebrity, then I'm too good for you.' he stormed off stage and the audience clapped and cheered for the first time.

We had quite liked him. He was unusual but he needed a different audience to the one he had. We went back to the caravan, pleased that all had become quiet again.

The lads had not returned. 'Maybe they've struck lucky.' I said to Miriam. She frowned. The thought that her boys were turning into men hurt her more than she wanted to admit.

Almost randomly I said to Miriam, 'That guy said he was a celebrity. I've never heard of him.'

Miriam was getting serious as the alcohol wore off. 'Most celebrities are unknown in the longer term. They become kings and queens for a day. Their short-lived fame sells newspapers, films and CDs in the very short term before the fall into the pit of disrespect. Their fall sells more newspapers. You could almost do a life-cycle study on most, so-called, stars. They are a commodity that is bought and burnt out like fireworks. All for the pleasure of the onlookers. We are all voyeurs.' Miriam repeated my thought from our first day on the beach.

We noticed that Dwayne Crokum was packing his equipment into the back of his station wagon parked opposite our temporary home.

Miriam shouted, 'Hello, great act. You are a misunderstood star.' Her sarcasm was missed.

His Southern drawl mumbled back. 'Thank you. Celebrities and Stars. Who needs them? I have been trying to make it for the past thirty years and all I get is an audience that doesn't understand basic English.'

He continued throwing speakers and cables into the back of his wagon.

'Got the idea for Dwayne when I visited Nashville donkeys' years ago. I wondered how so much could have grown from the base of women leaving men, men being unfaithful and dogs dying. Nonetheless, it's good music. Reckon it's because it's got emotion. People can sympathise and empathise with the songs. It's all happened to everyone, especially me.' Dwayne gave the impression that he was only speaking to himself. He was almost thinking out loud. He probably kept himself company during his drives from show to show.

'To make it in music nowadays you need to look good. Young pretty girls and handsome men are the ones that ride the merry-go-round. There again, I guess it was similar in other times when men were rugged, like Elvis and Johnny Cash, or were feminine like Dolly. Now it's about young strips of lookers with electronic music that could make my cat sound like an opera singer. You need a big chest to hide a small voice. Yeh! I guess I am bitter and twisted.'

I whispered to Miriam, 'Let's walk along the sand in the moonlight. We haven't done that for years.' I grabbed her hand and we strolled towards the beach.

We walked away from Dwayne and he did not even seem to notice. We only laughed at him when we felt we were out of earshot. I said to Miriam, 'Basic English. I am a native English speaker and I found it difficult to understand him.' We laughed so loudly that we were sure Dwayne must have heard us that time.

The celebrity cult reflects the need to feel good about ourselves by association with others who have done better. We love to build actors, pop-stars and television presenters only to glory in their falls. We make them gods and watch as they plummet like falling angels onto the rocks that smash them.

Yet the real stars were bright in the dark sky. Their light seemed to be reflected by the mass of tiny shells that sat on the damp sand at the water's edge. Perhaps it was the wine, but I could imagine the beach to be the sky and the sky to be beneath my feet. There was a sense of silence in the night, which was an oasis in the continuing noises of modern life. We were away from the constant roar of automobiles and the ever present sound of jet engines overhead that we got at home.

Those interruptions had ceased to be at that point of time in our Paradise. The movement of the sea as it reached to caress the beach sounded like the planet breathing its sighs of resignation to the attempted domination by mankind. I stood, holding my wife's hand, watching and listening for as long as was needed to make me feel that I was of no more importance to the Universe than one of the shells on that beach. Surprisingly, I found the thought to be reassuring.

As a child I had been intimidated by the power and seeming eternity of the sea. The waves were powerful and could wreak so much destruction when they were angry. They must have travelled the whole ocean in search of a cliff or beach to die on. They had so much pent-up energy that could be spent as a caress on a swimmer or as total destruction in a tidal wave.

The love I had for Miriam was so strong at that moment. It was emotion rather than lust, but as we kissed there was a growing desire in my body.

We sat on the sand for a few moments before a spotlight picked us out. There was loud shouting in Italian. We wondered what was happening. Then a man with a torch arrived. We told him we were resting. He then told us in poor English that it was forbidden to lay on the beach at night.

'Why?' I shouted at him. 'What do you think we are doing?'

He explained that it was for safety. We did not understand. We were being expelled from the beach for something as trivial as an embrace. I wondered what danger lurked on the sand at night, anyway.

With my pointless threat of complaining to the management, we left.

As we walked back to the caravan we burst out laughing at the sight of two lovers hiding in a sand hole dug by some children during the day. It reminded me of trench warfare.

'Make love, not war.' I called to them as we passed. Miriam pulled my hand as if to get me away from any reprisals from the couple who had just experienced coitus interruptus.

The lads were home when we got back. They complained that they were told not to drink beer in public and that they had not met any interesting folk while they were exploring.

We explained in a discreet way what had happened to us. Even so, they looked embarrassed at the thought of their parents doing what they would have liked to have done that evening.

So drinking in public and cuddling in the dark of the night were forbidden in this place. As Adam and Eve discovered, Eden has rules.

CHAPTER SEVEN

AT YOUR SERVICE

sunday

Sometimes, when one of the fish became ill, it would be taken up by the Net-of-God. Perhaps it might return, but usually it did not. A lot of time was spent discussing what happened to the fish that were taken by God. Were they put into a huge pond free from aliens, where food would be abundant and the water fresh and well oxygenated? Or were they tortured and kept in a small plastic bag like the ones that were seen sometimes when new fish arrived? There was no way to know. It was assumed, however, that the fish that had been good were more likely to be placed into the blissful world, and those that had been bad...well.

Hung-over and feeling delicate, I made my way to the toilet block where I showered, shaved and attempted to wake up. The reflection looked older still, so I ignored it. Miriam had reminded me that we had promised to go to church to repay our debt of honour to the vicar. This meant tidying myself up and wearing long trousers rather than shorts. Even this church would not welcome the sight of flesh.

Breakfast was slow and painful. Mark and Nick were tired and quiet. They refused to go with us to watch Walter Evans perform his professional duties. That was a strange thought. He was paid a salary for spreading the word of God and for reassuring his congregation. There again, he needed to live. It might be a vocation but his employers had to house and feed him.

Walter's wife, Jane, was ushering people into their seats. She put us at the front for some unknown reason. She stood next to her husband at the beginning and offered presents to the five, or so, children. She moved to the back of the church and met the rush of youngsters. She gave each of them a little sticker to go on their clothes.

As Walter began I felt tired and my attention drifted to

the architecture of a tailor-made multi-denominational building. I noticed that it was for the differing Christian sects rather than encompassing all religions.

Then the cabaret came on. A small lady who was approaching her mid-sixties was going to read the lesson. She was the most entertaining person I saw on that holiday. In quiet, almost whispered, tones she started.

'And a great storm of wind arose, and the waves beat into the boat, so that the boat was already filling. But He was in the stern, asleep on the cushion; and they woke Him and said to him..."

Her voice rose to a mighty shout, 'Teacher, do you not care if we perish?"

As the words echoed around, Miriam nudged me in the ribs, trying to stifle her laugh.

The reader's voice became quiet and gentle again. "And He awoke and rebuked the wind, and said to the sea..." This time we were ready as she roared, "Peace! Be still!"

I snorted.

Quietly once again, she continued "And the wind ceased, and there was a great calm. And he said to them..."

We could see the woman filling her lungs, "Why are you afraid? Have you no faith?"

We sniggered, resulting in a strange look from Walter.

Then her soft voice eased out the last part of the text in a mysterious way. "And they were filled with awe, and said to one another, 'Who then is this, that even wind and sea obey him?'"

It really deserved a round of applause, but there was silence as the congregation was expected to draw the meaning from the parable.

The rest of the service was an anticlimax and as we eventually made our way out into the square we noticed the figure of Annan walking from the church in the direction of our van.

We were feeling holier than the other holiday makers who were wandering around in their shorts but slightly sinful at our response to the little lady's best attempts to bring her message across in such a dramatic way.

'And lo, so it comes to pass that Annan is sitting in at the table.' Miriam sarcasm was suited to my feeling of foreboding.

'Did you enjoy the service?' He asked.

'We didn't realise you were a churchgoer, Annan. Were you coerced into attending by our jolly vicar as well?'

'I like to pop in now and again. Christianity is such a strange faith. It is full of contradictions. There is but one God. Then there are Jesus and Mary and the disciples and then the Saints and so on. Then there is the Holy Spirit...'

'The fizz in Coca Cola!' I interrupted.

Although he raised his eyebrows, Annan ignored my comment. 'Every faith has multiple deities, it appears. Hindus have Gods for different aspects of existence. Then the Egyptians did, and the Greeks and Romans. Every culture gave life different facets. Spirits have been an integral part of faith since the cavemen. Shamans believe that every life form has a spirit. Animism attributes spirits to inanimate things like rocks. Christians want you to believe in one God and then give three options for the same thing, the Trinity. Catholics add the Virgin Mary to the mix, perhaps to give a feminine and maternal figure to comfort us in a faith that otherwise diminishes women.'

'A glass of wine, Annan?' Miriam chipped in, more as an excuse to leave the scene for a while than as a gesture of hospitality. Perhaps she wanted to demonstrate her feelings of being diminished. Annan had been directing his diatribe at me, after all.

'Thank you, but no. Far too early.' He replied.

'I will, please.' I called out. I thought I would help her out.

I reached into my pocket and took out a pack of cigarettes. Feeling guilty, I lit one.

As if he was my father when I was a young teenager, Annan tutted and said, 'I'm disappointed in you Gee. I thought you were going to stop. It has been a day of disappointment. Did you see the faces on the children in church when they were offered a present and received a little sticker? That to me is the essence of religion. You are promised something that sounds substantial only to receive a let down.'

Not really knowing why, I was feeling angry with this

man who was preaching. I felt irritated so I started a skirmish. 'Who are you, Annan? You have been around us since we first started our holiday. Now I feel as if I am being told off by you and that is upsetting me quite a bit. Do I owe you something?'

Annan was quiet for a few moments and then looking straight into my eyes, began. 'Gee. I am old enough to have seen and experienced many things. The world has been kind to me and I believe that I am part of the planet, the universe and all the life that exists there. I am like a lake that has received water at one end and I have released it at the other. In that way there has been a flow of the new in me and I know that while the lake may look the same all the time, it is renewed by giving as well as receiving. If the lake holds onto its water with a sense of greed, it becomes stagnant. It is full of nothing but rot and decay.

'I am not on a mission to change you, Gee, but I am offering you some escape from the torpid state you have got yourself into. We agreed that you are stressed, you smoke too much, you drink to excess and you are overweight. Your show of annoyance just now is just another sign. There is not a single life insurance company that would cover you as you are.'

He had silenced me. He took his advantage.

'I am offering you a chance to live as you should. You care for people, I know. You helped my daughter when she had big problems. You enabled her to look into a future that she did not recognise that she had. Before she came to you she had made three attempts to kill herself. Now she is a wife, a mother and the provider of my grandchildren. I want to repay you for all that. I want to help you to stop killing yourself in a more insidious way than swallowing sleeping pills. When we met on the plane it was coincidence, perhaps fate, but I recognised your name. When you told me where you practice, I knew it was you. I made some phone calls to confirm that it was you. Then I asked my driver to follow you here and I booked into the hotel to be nearby. I checked your background. That's how I knew about your family. You are a good man with a wonderful wife and two bright sons.

'Have I answered your questions and satisfied your

curiosity, now?'

I was dumbstruck, as was Miriam who was standing in the awning with a bottle of wine in her hand. She had overheard everything. I extinguished my cigarette and apologised for my behaviour. Annan reached for my hand and shook it warmly. 'Now we can become friends.' He said with a smile.

'Should I put this away?' Miriam asked meekly.

Annan answered for all of us. 'No, we will all have a glass, but not too much. We have work to do this afternoon. Usual place, yeh?'

At that point, our sons surfaced from their beds, requested that they go wind surfing later, and ambled to the shower block.

'Isn't it strange that they take showers before getting wet in the sea later on?' I commented as Annan left and we started to make some lunch.

'Well, what a surprise!' Miriam was intrigued by what had happened. 'So you saved his daughter from killing herself.'

'I cannot remember. It must have been a good few years ago. She has children now, so it was a long time ago.' I muttered.

I felt flattered that I had been of use, however. I remembered few of my clients. To remember people means becoming involved too much in their troubles. I had to remain dispassionate and objective. Offering unconditional positive regard means exactly that. Once a therapist becomes conditional then opinions have to be formed. At that point clients become more than strangers who need help, they start to attack the neutrality of the therapist.

Salami, bread and peaches consumed, we prepared to move our bodies to the beach. We found that our space had been invaded by a family of Italians. 'Of course, it's Sunday. All the locals are having a weekend break. Wish we'd left our towels here, yesterday.' I moaned.

We set up our base-camp nearby so that Annan could find us. Armed with Euros, the young sailors moved along the beach to the wind-surfing centre. Miriam and I spread our bodies on our towels and embraced each other for awhile. We knew that it was acceptable to have contact during the day on the beach. Yet it was too hot so we parted our sticky bodies and dozed.

When Annan arrived I did not feel the same negativity that had struck me each time before.

'Where are your fine young men?' he started.

'Somewhere out there.' Miriam pointed to the sea. 'Over there by the look of it.'

Two sails were close to each other. The aim of both lads seemed to be to capsize the other brother.

'A life on the ocean wave.' I added, needlessly.

'I love waves.' Annan was never lost for words. He had a view on everything, it seemed. 'Waves are at the foundation of everything. Nature seems to abhor straight lines and goes out of its way to add curves to all things.'

'Especially the girls on the beach.' I wanted to gauge his reaction to women. His comments about our 'fine young men' worried me at a very basic level. I wanted to confirm that he was a heterosexual man. Professional checking, I guess.

'Especially the girls on the beach.' He replied, gazing at Miriam. I was reassured but, at the same time, made uncomfortable that it might be my wife he was after.

'So, where shall we start? And how much should we tackle in each session? May I suggest that we begin by getting you to breathe correctly? Again!' Annan emphasised.

He repeated what he had told me the previous Wednesday; diaphragmatic inhalations, holding, exhaling and pausing. Both of us were equipped with our piles of sand and we practised until we were nearly asleep. Not through tiredness but from relaxation.

'That is good.' Miriam commented. 'It should be used as part of an anti-stress routine.

'It is.' Annan smiled.

'Imagine that you have a nozzle inserted into your navel. If you look at a petrol pump nozzle you will see that it has a little pipe that theoretically vents gas vapours. Imagine that when you breathe in you are inflating your bodies to the five points at the extremes, namely the top of your head, the tips of the fingers on both hand, and the tips of your toes. It might be easier to start by concentrating on them individually at the beginning and then amalgamating all of them when you are used to the feeling.'

We did as instructed for an immeasurable length of time. We were just enjoying the moments as they slipped away.

'Not only does that relax you, but it also gives you the escape route from smoking, Gee, as we discussed before. Do it.'

'Where on Earth did you learn all this, Annan?' Miriam was curious.

'Almost everywhere on Earth.' His cryptic reply was wistfully given. 'Let me tell you about rhythms and waves. There is very little that exists without curves and rhythms. From the structure of the atom through to the design of the cosmos, those two things give life. The movement of the wind and the sea depends on waves of energy. That energy is being borrowed by your sons at this moment.' Annan looked to the sea to locate the sails.

'The breathing exercise that you did was a rhythmic wave that put oxygen into your blood that was pulsed through your bodies by the beating of your heart. And, as you know, Gee, the brain has different waves; beta, alpha, delta and very importantly for relaxation, theta. That is the wave that predominates when you are relaxing. It is what helps dreams when you are asleep. It is the explanation for hypnosis and meditation. It is also what occurs in sympathy with the drum of the shaman.'

'Is that what you are, Annan, a shaman?' I wanted to take every chance to discover more about the man.

'No, I am not.' He seemed affronted. 'I am too rich to be one. A shaman is made by his history. To be a shaman a man has to learn from the moment of his birth. A doctor can learn about surgery and pharmaceuticals in seven years or so. A shaman's art has to come from his belief, his heart of emotion rather than from his head and hands. I have been lucky enough to have travelled to most of the planet in my professional career. I was fortunate enough to have been able to write my own itineraries. I would organise business trips to include time with the older cultures of each continent. The aborigines of Australia, the native Indians of North and South America. The tribes of Africa and the Siberians and

Eskimos. Those varying cultures are all tied together by the same approach to healing, an approach that is at the heart of psychotherapy. They are the principles that were adopted by Carl Gustav Jung. And at the centre of their beliefs is the idea that the world is a living thing. The concept is that the planet is alive with energy and spirits. Their relationship with Mother Earth is a symbiotic one where each party helps the other. Our twenty first century approach of so-called civilised people is purely parasitic. Men extract the life from the Earth, they cut down rain-forests, pollute the oceans, and drain oil to burn with nothing given in return apart from negatives. Global warming comes from laziness and greed. Cars, factories and so on.

'We live a nightmare. We are balanced between the new masters and the old slaves. People working every hour to build luxury items for the Western markets at low cost. People are used like machines in factories that have no safety rules. They use toxic chemicals that strip life away from workers who get nothing in return. Animals are killed to extinction for their skins. Forests are stripped to make furniture. Drug barons sell humiliating deaths for money. People are murdered for profit, and I include tobacco companies in that group of thugs.

'Most people seem to use the spiritual path for their own benefit. I have wondered about monks who sit and pray for hours in order to achieve their own peace with God. The modern preachers are pseudo-healers. They sell concepts of ritual to folk who want to find peace. They teach that we should look outwards to find God and inwards to find our faults. They need to turn the idea on its head. God, the Universe is within us and the problems are outside in the world. By caring for the world and its suffering we come to terms with our inner conflicts by default. Instead, priests make us frightened of retribution. Pseudo-shamans take our money for spells. The real shamans were, and are, healers of people, animals, plants and the planet. They gave their souls to save others. They took the risks of travelling into the world of evil spirits that, today, would be the psychoses of psychotics, to help alleviate suffering. They never did it for material gain. It was never the way it is now. Civilisation takes from the life of the world for short term gain. We need to experience the world rather than possess its assets. Rather than having, we need to be. We make ourselves miserable by striving to have more than we need. As a result of personal greed we are killing our planet; we are strangling our mother, the Earth.

'My hope for an afterlife is not being in a Heaven full of do-gooders who have earned enough bonus points, nor to be reincarnated as another human who has to win or lose depending on where I am born. I like to think that all my experiences and emotions will float out of me at the point of my physical death. Call it my soul, if you want. I could then travel the planet as an invisible bubble at the mercy of breezes. I could see the beauty that is our world; the mountains, the forests, oceans and all the life there is that has not been destroyed.

'Anyway. I guess I'll have to wait to see what happens when my time comes.'

Miriam and I watched in surprise as we saw tears slowly running down Annan's cheeks. He was not embarrassed, but pained at the fate of our beautiful world.

Annan wiped his face with his hands and changed the subject. 'OK. Let's continue talking about weight and shape.' He was addressing both of us even though I had not been part of earlier discussions.

Miriam moved to sit in front of Annan like a young girl at school.

He started as if acting in a Shakespearean play. 'What I love most about my body is its perfection. The systems work beautifully without me having to think about anything. My heart pumps, I breathe, I digest, my temperature is controlled better than the average air-conditioning units and my hormones are measured and balanced without me having to lift a finger. And I could go on and on. I think that I am a perfect self-regulating capsule of flesh, nerves, bone and blood.

'We would be very boring if we were all robots like the Stepford Wives. And as my body looks after itself, then I have the time to do the more enjoyable things in life such as eating, drinking and loving. Some of our bodily activities, like breathing, are semi-automatic. Others such as temperature control may be assisted by wrapping ourselves in warm clothes or throwing ourselves into a pool, river or ocean. We sometimes feel like passengers in those life-supporting bodies. We relish the external world through its smells, tastes, sights, sounds and feel. That is why I am perfect. And so are you. Your body works in the same way as mine.'

We were startled by this lack of modesty. Miriam and I looked each other. Annan caught the look that he had been waiting for and continued.

'However, for every yin, there is a yang. For every minus there is a plus. Many years ago, what I hated most about my body was the excess fat that put my blood pressure up and threatened my good life by clogging my arteries. What disturbed me was that sense of panic and stress that seemed to run my life. As life-forms, we demand balance. As people we hope for relief from our problems.

'In the beginning we were a species that wanted to live. We needed to survive in order to avoid the pains of death. Most of all, we wanted to enjoy the pleasures of mating and, consequently, rearing the next generation.

'However, our world was full of creatures that saw us as nothing more than a herd of animals that tasted good and were easy to catch. Some creatures found us to be a threat and developed venom. We had to learn how to avoid the snakes and spiders in a rapid way. One mistake and we were dead. In this, nature was a great ally. It provided us with exquisite tools for survival. Life was simple and sensuous even if short because we lacked medicines in a beautiful, but deadly, Eden.

'In our modern and comfortable worlds we still have those tools that kept us alive for hundreds of thousands of years, those internal systems, senses and emotions over which we assume we have little control. They are beyond our conscious bidding. They can cause us to panic. We can develop fears and sometimes we feel unable to control our bowels. Somehow we feel driven to store more fat than we need. And, as those systems seem to be unrestrained we feel incapable of having any influence on them.

'Anxiety and corpulence behave like delinquents. It is

true that direct intervention is unable to help, but we are able to persuade, coerce and trick our bodies and minds into doing what we want. We are able to survive our survival systems.

'Fat storage is a wonderful survival system but we need to know how to control how much we hoard. And that is easy.'

He paused and waited for the return of our attention that had wandered.

'We are told that we have five senses, namely sight, hearing, touch, smell and taste. They are the ones that we are familiar with. They enable us to become aware of the world outside our bodies. They allow us to become acquainted with our environment.

'We actually have more than those five. The others are the inner senses. They are the ways in which our bodies experience and regulate themselves internally. For example, we have a sense of balance. This is the sense that tells you which way-up you are. It is the one that gives you a feeling of movement, direction and orientation when you are in an aircraft.

'Then there is another sense that is used in re-setting your body-shape-blueprint. It is called proprioception, which gives you information about where you are in space. It gives you an internal perspective. This is your sense of proportion.

'Extend the first finger on your right hand, extend your arm to the side, close your eyes and then touch the end of your nose with the extended digit.

'Which sense did you use to find your nose? Not sight, your eyes were closed. Not taste, not smell, not hearing. You did not even feel it until you made contact with your nose.

'Without moving or touching yourself, feel the sole of your left foot. You are sending slow nerve impulses to the sole of your foot so that you can verify its existence. Signals are then sent back to tell you that it is there. It is like using radar to detect something and then to pinpoint its location.

'Again, without moving or actually touching yourself, feel where your right hip is. Now feel where your left hip is. Now feel the space between them. This body checking is going on all the time, but at an unconscious level. However we can switch our conscious thought into it at will. We can feel our shape within our own mind.

'Now, with your eyes closed and without touching yourself with your hands, use proprioception to feel the fat on the back of your upper arm as it is as if you were kneading dough. Now feel the shape of that part of your arm as you would like it to be.

'This is the insight to weight and shape control. Presume that the feedback goes into a processor, which checks against a blueprint and then changes our system to maintain our shape. Of course, our blueprint cannot be seen in a person's brain, but it can be seen within our mind's-eye or, for some people, felt with the mind's hand.

'The good news is that we can consciously change our blueprints, and when that is done, our bodies will change their shapes.

'You become aware of every part of your body bit by bit from the shape you are now to the shape that you would like to be, within reason. Within reason is important because the mind and body work for survival. Remember that super-model shapes are for selling clothes, not for copying! If you see or feel yourself at an unhealthy body shape, you run the risk of problems.'

Annan prepared to leave us practising our new weight control method.

'Excuse me, I'll see you tomorrow.' He turned to go.

'No. We are going to the Water Park with the boys. How about tomorrow evening? Come and eat with us. Is seven o'clock all right?' Miriam was looking upset that he was going.

Annan answered with a nod and with a final reminder to me to stop smoking and start breathing, he left.

CHAPTER EIGHT

CALMING THE WATERS

monday

God seemed to be too remote. He only seemed to answer prayers sometimes. For example, when the pond became hot in the summer and more oxygen was needed, the fish would go to the sky, look upwards to where God appeared to appear, sometimes, and they would mouth prayers for air. This didn't work every time. Some days the 'thing-that-gurgled", as it was known, didn't work, and the fish felt choked. Sometimes it sucked young fry into itself for its nourishment.

I do not like theme parks very much. I am too old to enjoy the rush of adrenaline that is loved by people much younger than me. Whereas the beach was a place that had its own sounds, the Water Park was alive with screams, splashes and shouts of bravado that made relaxation somewhat difficult. I was there simply because it was easier than being absent. We had promised the lads something which they had requested to do, so I sat on a towel on the grass, worrying about the millions of ants that must live in their own paradise of sugar from spilled soft drinks, and crumbs from sandwiches and burgers.

I had started to breathe without the prompt of a cigarette and I felt good. There was something to what Annan had said, after all.

The major downside of sitting around was that I started to think.

The park was different to the beach. I was 'people-watching'. Here the mix was totally changed. There were far more teenagers who were undergoing their public rites of passage. The adolescent sense of immortality allowed them to take the apparent risks that were required to impress their peer groups. Logic told me that the risks were well within actuarial boundaries. Theme parks offer danger that is actually completely safe. They have to or they would have no customers.

'Come on dad' was a constant demand from the boys. Miriam joined them. 'Come on Gee, they're only young once. I'm going on the big drop with them later on. Join in. you are acting like an old fuddy-duddy.'

'That's because I am.' I protested. 'Maybe later on.'

I got my notepad out of the beach bag that we had brought and started reading. I liked keeping notes when on holiday. They would take on a new flavour when reviewed years later. It was like laying down bottles of wine to mature.

I wrote some diary pieces as well as I could remember. The visit to Venice and the islands, the panic I felt when I was at the top of the Campanile. I was unable to put down much about Annan, he had lectured and tutored, but most had sunk into parts of my mind that had left an impression rather than substance that could be regurgitated.

I did my best to remember Annan's daughter. I cast my mind back. She would have been Asian in appearance. She would have been troubled if she had made three suicide attempts.

There was a glimmer of a memory that started to shine. I wanted to contact my office to dig out my notes but they were securely archived. Only I had access and I realised I did not even know her name. I wondered about the causes of self-harm. Intolerable emotional distresses connected to abuse, bullying, lack of self-worth and revenge.

I gave up trying to remember an individual case.

Miriam would not stop encouraging me to join in. Eventually we set off together, grabbed a small rubber inflatable raft and climbed endless stairs to the departure point. The raft enabled the two of us to sit one in front of the other, and launch into a stream of water that would take us down a series of curves before dumping us into a pool at the bottom. Before agreeing to Miriam's constant nagging, I had watched others descend. It seemed to be within my range of coping skills. They gripped the rubber handles and smiled on their way. Most even laughed when they had finished.

Just before we started our white water journey, I tempted fate by repeating the words we had heard in church yesterday. 'Peace! Be still!'

Fate rewarded me with troubled waters and G-forces that were more suited to a NASA astronaut than to a middle-aged therapist.

The splash at the bottom felt more of an explosion as I disappeared beneath the surface and one of Miriam's legs made contact with my head.

'Let's do it again.' She pleaded. Words that I had not heard from her for a long time.

'Later.' I snapped. I wanted to return to the safety of my towel and the warmth of the sunshine.

After a while, the cajoling started again. This time we climbed onto a longer raft. I was at the front with my legs over the low bow. Miriam was at the back with her legs around my thighs. I gripped the handles and we went onto the ride that took us down the inside of a completely dark tube illuminated only by tiny lights above us. We hurtled along taking unseen sharp turns and sudden drops that added to my alarm until I was so petrified that I wanted to escape. There was no way out or off and my body became tight and tense. I feared a heart attack for the third time on that holiday. The ride got faster and steeper until we burst into bright sunlight that blinded me temporarily after the blackness. We skidded across the surface of the pool until I managed to bowl a young boy over with my feet. He had been waiting to claim our raft for his turn.

My breathing was tight and rapid. My chest felt as if it were going to burst. At the same time I felt dizzy and faint. I grabbed Miriam's arm and she helped me onto dry land.

After we had returned to the cluster of towels, I reassured Miriam that I was going to live and flopped down on my back. I wanted a cigarette but I had none. I started to breathe as Annan had shown me, this time using two Bottles of water as my weight. After a short time I felt much better, the panic was easing away.

Miriam watched and ensured that I safe. She told the boys that I had felt tired and they went on their perpetual quest for a water ride that would challenge their flow of testosterone.

'You should see a doctor when we get home.' Miriam was worried by the episodes of panic that I had suffered in

Italy. 'It might be that you are dehydrated.' She added. 'I haven't seen you drink much water. You have drunk wine, most of the time.'

'I am fine. Anyway wine is good for you.' I said.

'You had two litres of water on your stomach. Drink some of it now. It will make you feel better.' At times, Miriam reminded me of my mother when I was a child.

I drank some to please her, even though it was lukewarm.

'Are you coming on the big drop, dad?' The lads were eager to experience the scariest ride in the park. Girls screamed and men roared as they plummeted from a huge tower down a nearly vertical drop. It was too much for me but Miriam wanted to please her sons and reluctantly volunteered to go with them. I watched as they found a rubber raft and climbed upwards to the top. It was so high it took a long time for them to disappear from view on the platform from which they would be launched.

I saw the raft slowly edge its way into view. Miriam was at the front. Then the slow motion of the trio became a blur as they dropped. Rather than scream, Miriam shouted a string of swear words. Then they levelled out, shot along the gutter at the bottom before being dumped into a pool.

I walked down to meet them. Miriam was not happy. She described every moment in graphic detail. She vowed never to do it again. The boys looked sheepish. Too old to show their fear they covered the experience with bravado. They would never do it again, either.

Around four o'clock we packed up and walked to the bus stop. The lads were happy, but tired. Miriam was watching me more than usual which I found comforting. I think she had experienced the same feelings of panic as I had and she was empathetic.

Back at the Caravan Park, we did our food shopping for the evening and Miriam then set about preparing our meal. The boys volunteered to go out for a pizza. They wanted to escape the company of a man they thought to be at best, boring, and at worst, very strange.

'Do you think Annan eats the same food as us?' She worried. 'He is Indian, so he might be a vegetarian. I'll go back to the supermarket and get something else.' She virtually ran.

Cooking a meal for a guest on a grill with two gas rings sets a challenge, yet in a simple way, it makes life easier! French cuisine is based on peasant food in which it is necessary to extract flavours and nutrition from what is available. Chicken, or other meats on bones, are boiled up with a multitude of vegetables. Bread is cooked moments before being eaten.

Yet how did they manage to add foodstuffs that are so alien to the British? Perhaps the First World War and maybe other conflicts before it might have driven starving people to consume whatever protein was at hand. Dead horses would have been available after the cavalry mounts were slaughtered by machine guns. Snails would have been plentiful living on the detritus of battles. Frogs would have grown large on the flies and mosquitoes that bred in trenches. Obscene as those thoughts are, the need to survive in the midst of so much destruction would have been great. My thoughts removed my appetite so much than when Miriam returned I had no interest in her menu.

'I thought we would start with goat's cheese, tomato and basil on some of the French stick from breakfast. Then a tomato and aubergine sauce on pasta followed by fresh fruit.' She looked pleased with herself but disappointed with me. 'Is that not to sir's liking? You look glum.'

I replied that I had felt a bit queasy but her meal sounded delicious. Not a scrap of dead flesh to be found. Unless Annan was vegan, he should be delighted.

Miriam started to prepare. She refused my offer of help. This was going to be her creation. I sat and wrote my thoughts about French cooking in my diary.

Annan arrived on time. He brought with him a bottle of Italian wine and a bunch of flowers. Red and white blooms decorated by large green leaves. His diary was clasped under his armpit.

'God. He's going to make appointments for our sessions.' I thought.

Annan bowed to Miriam. 'The colours of Italy for a beautiful lady.'

Miriam kissed him on the cheek and said, 'Annan, you are so romantic. Gee never brings me flowers anymore.'

Women really are multi-tasked. A compliment for one and an insult for another, all in two short sentences.

'And for you, I have made our starter in matching colours.' Miriam was flirting by taking advantage of a coincidence.

Although I had partly lied to Miriam about feeling queasy thirty minutes before, my stomach churned. The only relief was the mime of being sick that the boys made behind Miriam and Annan's back.

'By the way. Are you vegetarian?'

Miriam felt it was safe to ask as she had taken her insurance with her choice of ingredients.

'Goodness me. No way! I love meat.'

I felt a little smugness creep into my heart. At least he would not be given something that he loved. This strange ambivalence made me wonder why I liked and disliked this man at the same time. I had a suspicion about him and his motives. I wanted to dig out his daughter's notes when I got home. They might hold a key to who this man really was. I needed to discretely find out from Annan what her name had been when I had seen her. Had he abused her? Surely not! If he had he would have kept his distance rather than living in our laps.

Miriam explained that she had prepared a vegetarian meal in case he did not eat flesh. Annan was excessively complimentary about her sense of consideration and foresight.

We sat at the table. To my surprise Annan sat opposite me rather than Miriam. He put his diary on the chair next to him, placed his phone on top and settled down. I poured three glasses of wine and opened bottles of beer for the lads.

This was to be our last supper, Annan announced. He was flying back to England to attend to some matters that had cropped up before travelling on to India, he explained. I was relieved to regain possession of our holiday and partially saddened at the loss of this acquaintance, perhaps friend.

I watched the lads pulling faces as they departed in

search of their suppers. I smiled back and Miriam waved. As they went, Mark tripped. Nick shouted out 'Throwback!' They scurried off.

Aware that the question would lead to a long dialogue, I had to ask Annan to explain what he was really about. 'Now that we are going to lose you, will you tell us more about yourself?' I wanted information about this man. It seemed to me that the chance meeting had not run its course. There was more to be found.

Annan sipped his wine, finished his starter and began. 'Not to offend your sons, but once, because of my colour, somebody called me a throwback. I was seventeen. When people describe others as 'throwbacks', what do they mean by this insult? We are, apparently biologically identical to our ancestors from tens of thousands of years ago. Rather than being throwbacks we are a species that has acquired a thin veneer of so-called civilisation, as you once said, yourself. We use that to over-value ourselves against other animals and human societies. The dawn of mankind as a modern creature was when a human made a tool for killing something. And so civilisation continued to develop. Language and social communication are perhaps not the preserve of humans. Listen to birdsong or wolves howling. The hiss of a snake says, "leave me alone, or else", and this is from a creature that is deaf!

'Perhaps the need to manufacture weapons came from our fundamental weakness and our powerful drive to survive. After all, we were born devoid of horns, claws, fangs, scaly armour and fur. This left us weak and vulnerable. Even the best Olympic sprinter could not outrun a lion. A heavyweight boxing champion could not put a fully grown gorilla onto the canvass. However, our weapons gave us a chance. A knife became a claw, a spear, an antler. We became able to strip fur from our quarry and wear it to keep us warm. Humans became able to change the world to their own design rather than having to adapt to the environment.

'And so our survival systems started to become redundant. We had systems that had kept us on this planet way before we developed weapons. We knew how to run away from danger. We knew how to forage. We knew how to hide. We were able to store fat to give us reserves of energy when times were hard. We had borrowed body hair to keep us warm.'

'Arse.' I thought. 'He's off.' Yet my thoughts did nothing to prevent him from going on.

'Sure, now some of us are hirsute, but most are nearly without hair. In the dawn of man, our hair was part of a sexual signalling system. The pubic triangle, now being trimmed in modern life, was a visual clue that we were in a breeding condition after puberty. Our few pieces of hair that were left held pheromones that acted as aphrodisiacs, or they grow long and bushy on the head to increase our appearance of size and importance. Now, paradoxically, men shave their faces and trim their locks while women shave their legs, pubic and underarm hair. Why? Women are encouraged to paint their faces to resemble the sexual signalling of our cave ancestors. Lips are reddened to look like aroused genitals. Breasts are lifted to make them look more milk productive and thus better for a prospective mate who wants to breed.'

I looked to see if Miriam was blushing. Instead she had a look of fascination at this story.

I was glad the boys were elsewhere. They would have been embarrassed by the references to body hair. Their obsession with hairstyles ironically made Annan's point about the value of hair in courtship.

'All of this is done in the name of fashion. All of this is to make us look different to our ancestors. Ironically, we use colognes, deodorants and perfumes to substitute for our pheromones. This makes us all throwbacks! Modern life has striven to modify facets of our nature. We are in denial of our primordial natures even though war is part of our historical and present lives. We hear news of rapes, murders, thefts and wars every day. We think we have control, but there is something deeper than our conscious-thinking that still runs us. They are the primeval killers that stalk us.'

He paused at last. Miriam and I were silent. We did not want to give him another feed line.

Annan sipped more wine as Miriam cleared our plates. She announced that the main course was fifteen minutes away.

'The person who called me a throwback, by the way, was priest at my school. He was a racist who taught in India because he wanted to convert the primitive people to his way of thinking. Hah!'

Professionally, I could see that although the wound had healed, the scar was large.

'I was expelled after I slapped the priest's face.' Annan smiled at the recollection. 'I am a pacifist, but even a vegetarian eats an occasional bug with his salad.' He laughed. 'He was a man whose only sense of freedom of choice was in allowing pupils to choose which leather strap they would be beaten with.'

'What did you do after being expelled?' I had to know more about this man's life.

"My father sent me to stay with an uncle in England. He was an entrepreneur who taught me how to find opportunities to make money. "Discovering the needs of people and fulfilling them for profit," as he put it. My uncle was a good man and his philosophy was that the needs must be genuine and that the fulfilment of them must be honest.

I got married to a girl that I loved. It was our choice rather than an arranged marriage. We had three children; two boys and a girl. She is the one you met.'

I wanted to interrupt to ask more about her so that I could find her in my files when I got home, but the moment was swamped.

'I worked in the supply of many things from food to housing. Twenty years after arriving in England I moved to America to stay with another relative. I used my skills to build small empires in many products. To my regret my family stayed behind while I travelled to and fro. My sons married and my wife, angry at my regular absence, found another partner while I was away. We argued, divorced and have never spoken to each other since. Her choice, not mine. For having so much money, I had nothing of any value. I had taken from the world and the world gave me back the dividend of loneliness and isolation.

'It worked out that I spent four months, on and off, of

every year in America with my businesses, four months, on and off, in England with my family who were running the business there, and that left me four months to travel, not as a tourist but as a devotee to the spirit of our mother, the planet.

Now one of my sons has moved to America and he controls the companies we have there and the other son runs what we have in England.'

'What about your daughter? What does she do?' Miriam jumped in before me.

'I do not know. She has two sons of her own, but we have no contact. After she came to see your husband, she seemed to be free from the devils that had haunted her for a few years. She met a man, married and then she sold her interests in my business and disappeared. I know that she is alive because she writes to her eldest brother by email, but she never gives me return address or phone number. I think she is living in India.'

Annan looked sad. There saw a hint of tears in his eyes for the second time.

'I thought that if I gave something back to the world then it might give me back my daughter and grandchildren.

As you treated her, I wondered if you could cast some light for me. That is why, when I met you on the flight, I thought that fate was giving me some help after all. Does she keep in touch with you, Gee?'

'No. I never encourage clients to have any contact after treatment. What is your daughter's name? When I get back I will try to find her file to see if I can help in any way. I must tell you, though, that I am bound by a promise to keep any information about my clients strictly in confidence.'

Annan nodded his understanding. 'Her name is Surrinder Singh, or it was when you met her.'

Miriam brought the pasta. As she put it on the table, Annan's cell-phone rang. He spoke rapidly in his Indian tongue.

'Excuse me, but I have to go. We will meet again. I apologise for having to go.'

He was agitated and shook my hand, kissed Miriam's cheek and disappeared into the night.

We sat dumbfounded. We lost our appetites in a flash and decided that we would have the pasta sauce for dinner the next evening.

'What the hell was that all about?' I asked Miriam. She had no more idea than I did.

After a while we started to clear the table. Annan had left his diary on the chair. I picked it up and leafed through it out of nosiness, to be honest. Rather than a diary, it was a notepad full of hand-written notes. I glanced at the contents and decided to read it the following day. Annan would be too far away to run after by now.

After we had finished the wine, the boys returned.

'We saw your friend earlier. Did you upset him? He was running and seemed to be crying. Then a big bloke grabbed him and they both ran to the main gate.' Nick had the delivery of a TV reporter at a disaster.

'No.' Miriam told him. 'He had an urgent call. Probably some business problem. How was your pizza?' The subject had been changed.

CHAPTER NINE

THE BEGUILING SERPENT

tuesday

The God figure was not seen at all, but nor were the spear-monsters. The solid sky offered protection as well as detachment. One day a beautiful fish arrived in the pond. It beguiled the others, but it was a predator. It waited until the other creatures began to trust it before starting to consume them, one by one.

Miriam and I woke fairly early. While she busied herself with some house cleaning, I sat in the bright sunshine. I had picked up Annan's notebook and started to read.

"The shamans and their cultures are the guardians of the Earth. And what is happening? Now I have seen, at first hand, how the aborigines and North American Indians have been corralled into settlements. Their credibility has been erased by the application of alcohol, something for which they have very little tolerance. It is an effective but savage to gain submission and control.
"Other cultures watch their habitats, the rain-forests and savannahs, being chain-sawed to the ground to provide furniture for the rich countries or stripped to grow crops for the Western consumers. Even India is being invaded by the all-pervasive need to become high-tech. The old beliefs will disappear. What we can surmise is that the true faiths are being buried by the new Trinity of Money, Luxury and Selfishness. I am returning to India to do something that I need to do. I want to free myself from having more money than I need. I want to live in the luxury of simplicity where only my basic needs for food and water are met. And above all I want to lose my self interest and give to others. It is wonderful that in India you can go to a remote village where the people have nothing. The first thing they will do is offer you food, even though they do not have enough for themselves. They will look after injured animals. That is the

essence of the spirit of life. The problems will start when somebody gives them satellite television. Then the villagers learn what they do not have and become unhappy. Because they watch the TV they stop talking. They joy of a simple life is yet again lost.

'There is a God, and that God is the essence of the Earth. God created the world and then man created God in his own image in order to usurp the very essence of God, the creator of beauty and balance. The mistake, or strategy, is that we have given God a human form, and that form includes our failings. God is the planet, the universe, life and creation. We have personified God as a superhuman. We need to learn that God is the spirit of life, beyond blame, beyond judgement."

'There are no dates in here. I've no idea when all this was written. But Annan is bizarre.' This was said to myself as much as to Miriam after I had read the first page of Annan's notes over a croissant and cup of coffee. 'He sounds like a new age evangelist. But he must have travelled a lot to see different cultures and to study them. The amateur anthropologist.'

'What did you say?' Miriam was preparing breakfast for the lads and she had been distracted.

'This stuff by Annan is interesting. He seems to have moved around the world in search of the old cultures. Not like the Egyptians and Romans, but the primal cultures.'

'Can I read it, Gee?'

'Later.' I started to read more. I held this book as if it were a present just for me.

The noise of the dismantling of our neighbour's awning took me away from Annan. The couple we had only spoken to once walked over to bid their farewells.

'It vas goot mitting mit you.' The man said with a look of satisfaction on his face.

'Me too.' His wife added.

'We enjoyed meeting you as well.' I lied. These people were total strangers. We knew nothing about them.

They smiled and walked to their camper van. We never saw them again.

I returned to Annan's writings.

"The Ten Commandments, the basis of Judeo-Christian culture, are the words that exhort us to live the line, but which break their own credo by the implicit threat of damnation to those who do not adhere to them. Sin is thereby defined as our true nature. Thereby deliverance is our acceptance of the nature of man within the organised crimes of civilised countries such as war and social divides. A nation can covet its neighbour's ass and commit murder, rape and steal during its invasion, mostly in the name of God. Sadly, God lets it happen and nobody pays a price. Instead of pretending that we are a modern species born with innate social grace, we should recognise that we still have old people living inside us who live in huts and caves. We should deal with our behavioural foes as our ancestors did. There are no special rituals, unless we want them.

"The mystique that bars us from discovery is the work of zealots and manipulators. The way to gain access to our thoughts is easy. I have learnt that all we have to do is to believe that we are connected to the Web of the Universe. It is within us as well as outside. We can only see the stars that are visible, but we can imagine the stars beyond. The Universe can only be seen by our imaginations. I cannot understand the ubiquitous concept of good and evil, anyway. If a bear takes a man, his family and friends would consider the bear to be evil and would want to kill it. The family of the bear, however, would think the man-killer to be good because it brought home food. Values of virtue can only exist in the minds of the judges, and that depends upon their point of view rather than a universal code of conduct."

My reading had changed from an interested spectator to that of a psychoanalyst undertaking a diagnosis.
'Are you ready to go?' Miriam was waiting. The boys had decided to go back to bed until lunch time. She stood impatiently with two towels and her bag of sun creams while I went inside the caravan to put on my swimming trunks.
Deliberately, I left Annan's notebook behind in the small cupboard that acted as a wardrobe. We strolled to the

beach, hand in hand.

Miriam smiled at me. 'It is good to be together for a change. No Annan, boys in bed, just the two of us.'

Miriam steered us to a different spot to our usual one. I took of my shirt and sandals and spread myself on my towel. Miriam laid out hers, took off her shirt and settled herself beside me.

'God, Miriam, you're topless.'

'You seem to enjoy looking at the other women. I thought I would let you look at me for a change.'

I felt jealous and aroused at the same time. Miriam's behaviour touched something that I did not recognise. In our earlier years, before we had children, she had sunbathed topless. That seemed to be natural. It was part of the symbolic baring of the body as her emotions grew. This holiday, as usual in front of the lads, she had kept her top covered. Now she had taken me to a different part of the beach and without hesitation, she had exposed her breasts to the world.

'Why are you doing this?' I was intrigued.

'Because everybody else is. Do you have a problem with it? If you do, I'll put my shirt back on.'

The sight of her rubbing sun cream into her breasts was making me feel lustful.

'Shall I do that for you?' I smiled.

Miriam knew that she was turning me on. She was enjoying herself.

'No. I am quite capable. Anyway, I want to match my tan while the boys are out of harm's way. Those white bits look silly.'

'Not to me.' I looked at Miriam, longing to be able to touch, but aware that I could not. That was the public taboo that had been broken by the lovers we had seen a few days ago.

'Look at that woman over there. New arrival. Totally white.'

It felt strange to be directed by Miriam to look at a girl who had just arrived on the beach. She was young and pretty. Her blond shoulder-length hair was pulled into a ponytail and tied with a band. She undressed to her underpants. She sat down and slipped her pants off, replaced them with bikini bottoms, spread a towel and commenced her worship of the Sun God. The brief glimpse of her trimmed, black, pubic hair had sent a shock through my body. A young man arrived shortly afterwards and sat down without speaking a word.

'I think you have looked enough, Gee.' Miriam was annoyed.

'Would you put some cream on my back please? If you can tear yourself away from the striptease show, that is."

At least I could now touch Miriam in an acceptable way. I deliberately positioned myself to be facing away from the girl in order to signal to my wife that I was not a voyeur.

She laid on her front while I applied her sun lotion. I found that I was scanning the beach. It was pure greed. I was caressing the body of the woman I loved and at the same time looking at people I would never talk to, let alone, touch.

When I had finished, Miriam rolled over and I lounged beside her. We held hands and snoozed.

After a while we woke and swam. We returned to our towels to dry. The young woman and her partner had gone.

When we returned to the caravan, via the shops, we had to wake the lads for lunch.

A new camper van had been parked in the space left by our German ex-neighbours. A bright and shiny vehicle sat in the sunshine like a swan posing on a riverbank. The number-plate told us that the inhabitants came from Austria.

After lunch we returned to our usual spot on the beach. Miriam had covered her breasts again and we had lost our youth once more.

I had taken Annan's book with me and I settled down to continue reading.

"There are two different ways in which things are spread. The first is infection and the second is fertility. One is about destroying anything that is different, and the other is for the renewal of life. A fungus which spreads by consuming everything in its path, and which is inedible, is an example of the first. It is selfish and therefore it is despised.

"Strawberries that spread by shoots and seeds are an example of the second. They give nourishment in return for propagation and every creature likes them. I have learnt that hate is like the fungus. It spreads for its own ends. It contaminates everything in its path. When the fungus meets an obstacle that it cannot consume then it has to make a choice. It can stay where it is and end up consuming itself, or it can change into something more friendly to enlist the help of other parts of nature. Perhaps that's what the edible mushrooms had to do. Remember we are all parts of something that extends below and above us. The strawberry plant can climb over the obstacle with a shoot as well as having its seeds carried away to a more fertile place by the creatures it freely gives its fruit to. Consider for a moment that perhaps the strawberry was a parasite before it became a giving food. Perhaps its change was forced upon it by circumstances.

"Now consider what is known already. Anger is a fungus and love is a strawberry. If we demonstrate love, then the repulsion that was felt for the fungus might change as well. People will remember the anger, but will appreciate the mushroom for giving rather than taking. But people are always wary of fungi because while some are nutritious, others can kill."

'Schizophrenic!' I said aloud.
Miriam jumped and replied, 'and you!'
'No. I am sure that Annan has delusions. He talks about God and mushrooms and strawberries as if they all exist.'
'They do, Gee. Perhaps it is you who has lost it.'
'I mean...he talks about them as if they are alive. Yes I know that they are, but mushrooms do not think anymore than strawberries do.'
Miriam grabbed the notepad and read the page I had left open while I sat quietly.
'Metaphors, Gee. You must know what they are.'
I was losing my drift. 'Of course I know what a metaphor is. I use them to help clients to understand solutions to problems. They encourage a different viewpoint. They enable lateral thinking.'

Miriam interrupted sharply. 'Not enough for you to turn the page. Look, it says, "story told to me by a shaman in Peru." He is relating a tale from a different culture. Stop being so hasty, Gee.'

'Do they have strawberries and mushrooms in Peru?' I asked sarcastically without expecting an answer.

Admonished, I went for a swim with the boys.

When I returned, Miriam had her head stuck firmly in Annan's notepad.

'This is not a diary. It is a journal of his travels. It tells stories that he has picked up whilst journeying. There is a lovely one about a cobra in India. Shall I read it to you?'

'No thank you.' I decided to ignore the contents of Annan's mind.

Miriam carried on reading. Now and again she chuckled. Sometimes she voiced surprise. When I asked her what she had read she refused to tell me. 'You have no interest in what is in here.' She pointed to the book, turned her eyes away and ignored me.

'OK. So tell me about the snake.' I was irritated that whereas Annan had gone in flesh, he was still with us in his never-ending words.

Miriam decided to relate the story rather than read it. It was her process of committing it to her memory so that she could tell others at home.

'There was a nobleman who enjoyed hunting. One day he shot and killed a snake, a cobra. He told his servant to drag it by the tail to the Tree of Life. This really does exist, apparently. It is a tall tree with big leaves that people use as canvasses to paint small pictures on. Under this tree, the servant was told to burn the snake. The belief was that the partner of the snake would come to the body of its mate, look into its eyes and see the face of the killer. It then seeks revenge. It was being burnt in order to prevent the snake's mate from looking into the dead snake's eyes. To ensure that the servant had followed his instructions, the lord went to the tree. He saw where the snake had been burnt. Suddenly, a cobra reared up and stared at the ashes for several minutes.'

'Can't you just see it, Gee, just staring?' She continued.

'The man reached for his rifle but before he could shoot, the cobra turned its head, looked quickly at the man, and then slithered away.'

Miriam's face showed me that she was describing a picture in her mind. She was there, under that tree.

'Many months later the nobleman was with his friends in the hills. They were hunting wild boar. One of the hunters took aim at a huge pig that was shuffling through old leaves while looking for food. Just as he was ready to pull the trigger, a snake lifted up its head and hissed. Shocked by this, the hunter discharged his bullet but missed the boar. Cries from a beater made the men run to the scene of panic. They found that the bullet had killed the nobleman and had passed through his body to kill the servant who had burnt the snake.'

'Bullshit. It's a fable. Snakes do not seek revenge. If that really happened, then it was a coincidence, an accident. Snakes do not mate for life.'

'You are a cynic, Gee. Why are you so dismissive of things? That story could be true. The point is that life is more than a series of logical events, cause and effect. Life sits on emotional responses rather than logic. For God's sake, you have been wittering on about how important emotional release is for your clients. You say that the key to resolution is in the...' Miriam was becoming angry and stopped to check her outburst.

After a few moments, she continued, 'Oh, to Hell with it. Some animals do mate for life. That has to be based on an emotional connection. The Golden Eagle keeps the same mate and will pine if its partner dies. If I died you would grieve for a while and then find another woman. The snakes and the eagles are more loyal than you. I reckon you are jealous of Annan's experiences, his money, his lifestyle and his charm.'

Miriam slammed down Annan's notepad and went for a swim.

I sat and thought about what she had said. Perhaps I was jealous of his success but not of his mental state. He was delusional.

When we returned to the caravan, a silence fell on the

four of us. Miriam was still upset about something that I thought to be trivial. The boys seemed bored, and I was restless. We have holiday dreams. We project how we will relax. We plan how we will feel. Yet the reality is that holidays rank high on the list of the causes of stress.

Perhaps I was jealous. When I had tried to tell Miriam about my thoughts in my own notepad, she had treated me as a madman. Now she was addicted to the notebook of somebody I considered to be insane.

My holiday had been transformed from my ideal into a tedious monologue in spoken and written words from a stranger. We only had his word that he was well off and successful. His stories of his life and travels could well be the fantasies of a schizophrenic. I had confirmed my diagnosis.

I lit the grill as instructed. We were going to eat steak and salad for our dinner.

I jerked as a mosquito buzzed past my face. I was desperate to lighten the moment. 'All this stuff about living in one world has made me aware that I am the father of millions of mosquitoes. The mothers suck my blood in order to breed. My genes are being absorbed into the insect realm. Those little buggers are going to be as brainy as I am one day.' My joke was received as poorly as Dwayne Crokum's songs.

'Hello.'

I looked for the source of the greeting.

A young man was walking toward me.

'Hello.' I replied.

'We are in the camper next to you. We arrived this morning.' He did not sound Austrian, so I wondered which new neighbour I was talking with. I wondered why he was talking about himself in the plural. There was no sign of his partner.

Miriam appeared, attracted by the arrival of a new man in the territory. She looked at him, put her hand out to shake his, and smiled. 'So? You have moved in next to us? Perhaps we can offer you a glass of wine. It is after six o'clock.'

'That would be nice. Let me get my partner.'

He disappeared into his camper.

'Nice looking guy.' Miriam said as she gestured with her eyes in his direction.

In the cliché of opposites attracting, Miriam was attracted by my opposite. Rather than being mid-height, mid-weight and middle-aged with thinning greying hair, this man was mid twenties, tall, slim and had a full head of dark hair. I started to dislike him immediately.

'His face is familiar.' I told Miriam, whose thundercloud had dissipated.

I went to find a bottle of our cheapest wine. I emerged with the corkscrew, four glasses and a litre of liquid that would be good for cleaning the kitchen stove.

Sitting at the table was the woman who I had seen on the beach in the morning. Miriam was back in her stormy weather mode. This was made worse when I headed back inside to find our most expensive brew, saying, 'Whoops, I've picked up the wrong bottle.'

'Hello. My name is Gee. This is...'

'We have already introduced ourselves. This is Adam.' Miriam pointed at the man. Her pecking order meant that she put him before the woman. 'And this is Lillie, his girlfriend.'

I shook hands with Lillie. I had met Adam five minutes beforehand so I nodded at him.

'So you are from Austria.' I told them as if they had forgotten.

'No, England. Ah! You saw the plates and saw we were driving an Austrian vehicle. We hired it. It was easier to fly to Klagenfurt and pick a van up there. It is not very far to drive. We want to tour Italy and hotels are too expensive. Hiring a camper van is an easier way to do it.'

Lillie had not spoken yet. She was very attractive, but this made me feel slightly uncomfortable. I knew from experience that men do not introduce their partners to men who could be competition. Either Adam was very confident with himself or I was too old, in his mind, to pose a challenge.

On the other hand, he was a rival for Miriam's attention. The boys joined us. Attracted like moths to a candle, they wanted to be close to somebody who would fit into their fantasies and they could then boast to their friends after the holiday. 'Yeh! She was a fit babe. Couldn't stop looking at me. We had a quick snog when her bloke went for a swim. Could have gone further but he came back early.' I guessed at the thought bubbles above their heads, perhaps projecting my own yearnings.

'Have you been to Venice?' Lillie spoke. Her voice was not silky smooth as I had imagined but was a little deep with a trace of a foreign accent.

'Yes. We went there last week and we will go again later this week, probably Thursday.' My body direction shifted so that I could look at her directly. I poured the wine and handed her the first glass. I kept getting flashbacks to seeing her naked on the beach. Here she was in the flesh, sitting at my table, sipping my wine. Here she was with her partner, my wife, my sons and they were all watching me as I made a fool of myself.

'Have you been to the beach yet?' My question put distance a between the voyeur and the man sat near her. It told her that I had not seen her body in all its glory.

'Yes. We went this morning after we had arrived. It is a nice beach but not very private. I felt that I was being watched while I sunbathed.'

While wondering if I had started to blush, I felt an imaginary kick under the table. I was aware of Miriam's unspoken sarcasm.

'What do you do in England? What is your occupation, Gee? Is it all right to call you Gee?' Lillie was being too polite.

'I'm a psychotherapist in private practice. How about you two?'

Lillie answered for both of them. 'Adam is a software engineer and I am a salesperson.'

'I work in an office.' Miriam wanted to be included. She took the initiative. 'What do you sell, Lillie?'

'Pleasure products. There is a high demand for self-indulgence in a stressful world.'

'Like toys and things?' I asked. I was curious.

'Yes toys.' She went quiet and glanced at Adam as if gaining his approval.

Lillie continued. 'Do you ever see famous people? You know, celebrities and stars?'

'Yes. From time to time.' I exaggerated. I had seen some minor luminaries, more like satellites than stars.

'Who are they?' Lillie was childlike in her curiosity.

'I am not able to say. Client confidentiality.' My face gave the appearance of holding deep secrets while Miriam's face gave a look of incredulity. She knew that I was lying about seeing famous people.

They finished their wine, made excuses, gave thanks and moved back to their camper van.

We cooked our steaks, made a salad and ate. Miriam was in a strange mood.

After the lads had gone for their evening search for beer and girls, I asked Miriam what was bothering her. I could see two things, Annan's notepad and Lillie. I wondered which was the central issue.

'That was the girl you were looking at on the beach this morning. Then you chatted to her in that slimy way that men have like a cat with a bowl of cream. That, added to your comments about Annan's gift to us and those derisive words of ingratitude, all of that has totally pissed me off.'

I suppose I had asked, so I could not feel as if I did not expect her onslaught.

My thoughts ran around. I wondered why she had been so upset about my reaction to Annan's stories. I questioned her reaction to Lillie when the meeting had been totally innocent. After all, she had been very coquettish with Adam. Certainly she had not seen his intimate parts but I had only glimpsed what was shown in a public place. Besides, he could well have been looking at Miriam's breasts. They were on display far longer than Lillie's pubic hair.

As if to please Miriam, I picked up Annan's notepad and started to read on.

"One of the most important things to develop is a sense of mystery. Not to mislead, but to do the opposite. Logic is a strong force that needs to be weakened before it will allow the imagination to work. The best way to do this is to show things that cannot be explained with simple logic. Trickery and illusions are known to be demonstrations of the slight-of-hand of the conjurer. They might entertain but they do not persuade. They can be shown to be exhibitions of skill but not of a special connection to the help of the Spirits.

"Magic, however, is a show of the affiliation of the wizard to powers beyond the reach of others. So if you can convince people that you have a special force, then you can generate their recovery. You will overcome their rational thinking and allow their minds to bring the cure. So magic is trickery done with greater skill than normal. But trickery that heals is not trickery for gain. When you eat certain herbs to relieve a problem, then you take it for granted that they will help you. Isn't it strange that there are medicines in things that are such a different form of life? Isn't it strange that those medicines have been found?

"If a Medicine Man gives somebody a mixture of leaves to chew and it cures an illness in their body, where is the slight of hand, where is the trickery? The medicines that are needed cannot be seen within the plants, but they exist. However the leaves have to be chewed to release their beneficial contents from the barriers that hold them in.

"When a spiritual medicine is given to cure an illness in a person's mind, where is the double-dealing? So, for us, we have to chew the barrier of logic away so that the benevolent actions of the imagination and thought can be released to heal. Developing a firm belief in your skills may be deceitful, but your power to heal is a reality. You can guide those thoughts to repair the damage from the harmful experiences that the sufferer carries. The magic is in everybody but it needs a catalyst to make it work."

This was very close to my professional practice. Rather than dismissing or analysing the words, I thought about them. I read the story about the cobra for myself. I then re-read the first few pages. Annan seemed to have skipped from Gods to spirits to life to herbalism. The references made about shamans gave me a clue. He had travelled to the old civilisations and had found a different level of life. There was a connection between his disdain of modern life and his need to know more about human life as it had been and how it was still present in the remnants of old cultures. And from what he had said, those old cultures were being destroyed by the empires of businesses, nations and organised religion. Our minds were humming the same tunes.

My profession as a psychotherapist was based on old techniques. Rather than pharmaceuticals, I used the process of allowing damaging histories to come to the surface, to be re-lived and then cleaning the wounds. Call the negative effects of abuse 'bad spirits' rather than unconscious conflicts and the resolutions 'drawing out the spirits' rather than catharsis and then the two are parallel roads. All that differs is terminology and methodology. Both involve emotional release.

Magic is the use of mental forces to bring about a change in the belief systems. The magic behind spirituality is the reason that it has been contained and made illicit by religions. As Annan had written, the magic to repair is in all of us.

Miriam came back to the table and sat down. 'I'm sorry, Gee. I feel a bit grumpy. Nothing that you have done. I suppose that all this stuff with Annan has been like a busman's holiday. You listen to people all day long. They tell you their problems and you help to get them better. Annan has problems in his life and he has been sitting on you like a weight.'

I reached for her hand, squeezed it and apologised in return. 'I'm sorry as well. There was no need for me to get upset earlier. I have been thinking about Annan's stuff and I think I can see where he is coming from. He has problems, certainly, but they are to do with his daughter and with the world. He goes from local to global in his mind. Perhaps he feels that one solution will fit all.'

Miriam was relieved that the brewing storm had been defused. 'As for Lillie. Well she is a child whose total world is contained in a toy shop. I suppose that Adam is a big earner and he needs his trophy bride on his arm. They are harmless enough. I don't think you two will have an affair or run away together. This is not like one of those films where the hero gets into a scrape every scene and is rescued in a bizarre way by a beautiful girl. Our lives are too ordinary for us to be involved in a mystery any bigger than finding what makes Annan tick and opening the next bottle of wine.'

'But she is a pretty young thing.' I had to add my comments.

Miriam then slapped my face. 'Got you.'

She wiped the flattened body of a mosquito off my cheek. 'Looks like I've killed one of your children.' She sniggered.

'Wiping the red mark, I told her, 'So, you liked my joke after all. That's not what I meant by a punch-line.' She grimaced at my pun.

I was aware that it had been a physical release of whatever she had been building up inside her mind.

I sat and looked at the mental picture of Lillie's body. I had seen more of her than most men. The exposure of her breasts and her pubic hair had been a secret I had been shown. I had a hidden knowledge that was made all the more exciting because nobody else knew. This was more appeasing than the answers that Annan sought. This was, perhaps, the perturbing recognition of the first awareness of a naked body that Adam had after Eve had eaten from the tree of knowledge. My thoughts had gone full circle to my first day on the beach.

'What are you thinking, Gee?'

My face was giving signs to Miriam that I was somewhere else.

'About the story of the cobra. It is charming, really. Get it? Snake. Charming!'

'Shut up, Gee.'

My alibi was completed.

An early night seemed to be a good idea, so after the boys returned, we went to the showers, washed and ten minutes later settled down in our beds. I wanted to make love but on this evening Miriam seemed inhibited by the proximity of our sons. My thoughts wandered in the direction of Lillie's body. This did not help me to dismiss my sexual urges.

Everybody in the camp must have heard the scream in the middle of the night. Blood curdling and violent, the noise drove Miriam and me to get up to investigate. It was so loud, even the boys woke.

Outside, it was quiet. No repeated howls to guide us.

'Do you think the young couple next door were fighting?' Miriam asked.

The lights in the camper van went on at that moment. The door opened and Adam came running out. 'Did you hear that noise? What is happening?'

He was off the hook. He wanted to help as well.

'We have no idea. We thought somebody was in distress and came to look.' Miriam was in charge.

We heard another scream. This time it came from the inside of Adam and Lillie's van. Adam rushed back inside.

Miriam and I returned to our beds. On the way we reassured the lads that all was well and that they should get back to sleep.

'What if there's a lunatic on the rampage?' Mark was being silly. 'There is only a sheet of canvass between us and a mass murderer.'

'Go to sleep, Mark. You would frighten anything away looking like you do.' His hair was dishevelled.

'You look beautiful, Mark.' Miriam had to protect the vanity of a young man. My words could have been misunderstood.

CHAPTER TEN

FORBIDDEN FRUIT

Wednesday

The plants in the pond were strange life forms. They were useful because they used the fish excrement as food, but that's why the fish thought them odd. They were also useful at making the water more breathable. But they were quiet. They had no worries at all. They were useful for offering hiding places from the aliens that sometimes slid into the water. Sometimes, some of the fish disappeared. Their screams were never heard.

'What are we doing today?' The question worried me. I had no answers for the boys.
'What would you like to do?' A question threw the initiative back at them. I was not a tour guide, after all.
'Can we go back to Venice? The last trip was spoiled by you freaking out.' Mark lacked subtlety. I thought he was getting his own back for my comment about his hair the previous night.
'What would you like to do, Miriam?' I needed an ally or a decision-maker to help.
'Whatever everybody else wants. I'm easy.'
'How about you, Nick?'
'Yeh. I'll do what everybody else wants.'
'What are we doing today?' I asked myself. My reply was equally as vague as all the others.
'OK. We'll do the beach today and Venice tomorrow. How about that?'
The decision decided and the grumbles grumbled, we bought, prepared and ate our breakfast.
By mid-morning we had moved to the shore, stripped, oiled and reclined. The two lads took their frustrations out on a football until one of the beach guards told them to stop. Apparently it was annoying for some of the other holidaymakers.
'Miserable sods.' I had become a grumbler as well.

We had travelled light to the beach. Just towels and a football. For some unknown reason I had picked up Annan's notes. I sat on the beach and started to flick through the pages looking for something that looked interesting. I saw the heading 'Journeys With The Shaman'. It was a long piece, but I had more than enough time to sit and read in the bright sunshine.

"I was finding that life and money were like opposing forces. The more of one that you have, the less of the other seems to be available. When I met the shaman, I had a feeling that I was going too be cheated out of both. This was my first visit to a North American Indian's village. I had been given a piece of paper with the name and location of a man who could possibly help me in my search. After travelling for three days by plane and car, I arrived in his village. It was too modern for my liking, and had all the appearances of being a commercial venture rather than a spiritual retreat. However, I wanted to go along with it all. At best I would find something, at worst I would have had a holiday that was different.
"I found the man's name unpronounceable, so he asked me to call him Jim! After I had settled into my quarters, he came to get me. 'How is your tepee?'
"I replied in a fairly sarcastic way. 'Fine, but it is a little too comfortable to be authentic, isn't it?' I wanted to make my point. 'What do you want? Rattlesnakes in your bed or buffalo charging through? It is to represent rather than be. It's the way it is. Unpack and settle down. I'll come to get you in thirty minutes.' He seemed to be a grumpy person, not a man at peace with nature.
"Just before he returned, feeling like a secret agent, I put my small mini-disc recorder into my pocket. We walked to a small fire that was offering nothing more than decoration to the scene. We sat on two blankets and my interview began. The following is the transcription of what was recorded:
"Jim started. 'Why have you come here? Many people visit this place in search of themselves. They often go away having found nothing that they did not have when they arrived. Are you looking for something that you have lost or

for something that you have not yet discovered?'

"I answered as best as I could. I explained that I had all the material things that I needed but I had not found...

"He interrupted and speculated. ' The meaning of life. Well, save your time and money. The meaning of life is written in a language that very few people can comprehend and you...'

I interrupted him back. 'No I am not looking for that. I want to find the spirits of life, not just for humans, but for the whole planet. The thing that I am searching for is the way to prevent men from killing our Mother Earth.'

A transition took place in Jim. I remember him looking at me. 'OK. Let's cut the New Age bullshit.' He said."

'Hello, Gee.' The sweet and innocent voice of Lillie brought me back from Annan's chronicle. 'We are going further up the beach where it's more private. We'll see you later. Come and have a drink with us this evening.' The couple wandered off. I regretted that we had camped in our usual space rather than the one where we had first seen Lillie and Adam.

Miriam scowled.

I thought that his booklet had been written for a reader rather than as a journal for the writer. The tone and style were the same as Annan talking to somebody else. I decided to skip the rest of the preamble and I turned pages until I found something meatier.

"After my request to learn the basis of magic, Jim said, 'Magic for change is easy if you have the special powers. I can make things change from one thing to another in just a few moments. Watch.'

Jim looked at my opening mouth with pride. He took a twig from the ground, held it in front of his own face and said a few incomprehensible words. He told me to hold my palms upwards. He then put the twig into the flames so that it caught fire. When it was burning brightly, he dropped it onto my hands. I jumped and cursed. I felt embarrassed at swearing in front of a Medicine Man. I then calmed down and apologised."

At least I had discovered where he had learnt the trick with Euro coin that he had given me. Create expectation and then fulfil it in a disappointing way. Back to the notes.

"Jim looked at me. ' Now we will have a long conversation.' he said whilst patting me on the knee as if to reassure me that they were still friends. 'If I change a fisherman's catch into venison, you might call that magic. If my wife changes the same fish into soup, you might call that cooking. If I change water and dirt into nuts then you would call that magic, but if a nut tree does the same thing you would call that nature. When I burnt your hand, I turned eager anticipation into calamity, I made an emotional change.'
"Feeling tricked by words that seemed rehearsed to represent the old Hollywood Indian model, but wanting to contribute, I said that if an apricot tree turned its fruit to pigeons, it would be magic.
"Jim made his point. ' But it wouldn't need to because the apricots will provide the nourishment for adult pigeons to breed, so the same result would be achieved. The problem with wanting magic is not so much in looking for spells or powers but in recognising the magic that is already available, everywhere. You and your wife made two wonderful sons and a daughter despite what was going to happen. You two were together and happy for long enough to do what was needed of you. The fact that you fell apart afterwards is neither here nor there.' I needed to hear more."

It seemed to me that Annan had borrowed more than just some of his ideas from the Medicine Man. It also confirmed that Annan and his wife had not had a happy marriage. I jumped back into the notes.

"It was at that point that I asked the real question that I wanted to be answered. I wanted to know if magic exists as something that a man can do to change others in order to bring about his own desires.
"Jim's dialogue sounded strange and confusing. I am

transcribing it as best as I can. A recorder records words and tones that a written transcript cannot convey easily. I know he deliberately attempted to get me to think in, what he called, different dimensions. He asked me to consider that the world he was in was paradoxically an imaginary place that he travelled to from one of the other worlds.

"He then asked if I had any proof that the world we were sitting on was the only one that existed. He proposed that other worlds were also real places but that our nightmares took place in this one. He asked me if it not seem strange that relationships broke down, children died, evil men possessed what they wanted and that nobody seemed to be fully content, here, on this lump of rock?

"Yet in the other worlds there were Spirit Protectors to help to resolve problems and they existed where our ancestors could continue to live because time did not exist.

"He asked me to consider the mad people of this world. Those, who because they seemed out of touch with a reality that had to be shown to be rational, were considered to be insane. Perhaps, he suggested, those people were living in the other realities and just visited here, in their minds, now and again in their seemingly coherent moments. Possibly, in their apparently irrational times, they returned most parts of their minds to the other world in which they lived."

Miriam's voice disturbed me at that point. 'Is it interesting after all, Gee?'

'Surprisingly, it is. There is a bit in here about a Medicine Man's view of madness that reminded me of a story that I had heard about the Government sending people to watch and listen to lunatic asylum inmates. They wanted to see if the, so-called, messages that were being picked up had any validity.'

'So did they?'

'No idea. I never heard the outcome.'

'Are you ready for lunch yet, Gee?'

'No. Let me finish this bit and then we'll go. By the way, I've found a bit in here about Annan and his wife having split up. I am intrigued to know why.' I returned to the notebook.

"Jim sat still and chose his words as carefully as he could. ' In the other worlds time does not exist as we think of it here. The only time that exists is the present. There is no future because the influences that create the future are in the here and now. If the present changes then the future changes as well.

"The past is a memory of how each point in time was. That cannot be changed because it has happened, and it therefore only exists in memories. Memories are only thoughts, and as thoughts change and mutate over time, then so will actual events appear to change as well. In this way the past that we know is only as real as a story. What do you remember from before you were born? Nothing more than you have been told, and that is not your experience, anyway. Stories are the thoughts of people that are changed and coloured to make them more entertaining, frightening or educational. We can never be sure that those stories are the truth. For now, the thing to be aware of is that the future is changed by the way we are in the present. It is not just changed by how we wish it to be, but by believing how we want it to be in the future. Wishing is a sterile hope. Wanting is a decisive action. The present is only represented by the change at that one point of time as the past moves to the future.'

"Then, he paused for a while. ' Remember the Universe is universal because it is the sum of every individual part. The Universe is in everything, so everything is in the individual. So the action, or inaction, of everything influences the individual. Therefore, the answers that you seek are in your own mind because the answers are in the Universe. Whichever way you look at it makes no difference. In the other worlds events pass like putting rocks into a quicksand. After a new rock has sunk, the surface still looks the same, but deeper down a change has taken place. In this world time passes like a horse galloping across a wilderness. Perhaps it starts in the East and travels to the West. The scene looks different from moment to moment, but the change is only on the surface. As all things are contained in the Universe and the Universe is contained in the parts, so all of time is made from moments and every moment contains all of time.'

"I remember Jim throwing a log onto the fire and saying, 'as we are in the part of the Universe where time is experienced, I know that we have had a long day. I am tired now.'

"He then left me to go off to his trailer telling me that he would see me at dinner."

I put the book down as if acknowledging the break in Annan's account. It seemed to me that Annan's wisdom was a replay of the knowledge of a wise man he had met in America.

'OK. Let's eat.' I felt as if I had woken from a dream. I was unsure about the meaning of what I had read. The medicine man was way above my conception of the world, yet I could follow his drift to an extent.

Miriam and the lads had waited patiently for me to finish. I had the feeling that they had been watching me as I read.

As we walked back to the caravan, Miriam asked me why I had become so interested in Annan's writings.

'I thought you had read this yourself.' I told her.

'I had a look but lost interest. It seemed to be a bit heavy and self-centred for holiday reading. Give me a good novel any day.'

'I can't summarise it for you. Read it when I have finished. It is very odd. Just like Annan.'

'The boys are bored. Shall we take them into the town, this afternoon?' Miriam sounded as if she needed a change from sunbathing herself.

I wanted to relax and continue reading. I was happy to isolate myself from all outside influences. 'You take them. I'll stay here and relax. Later, I'll cook dinner for us all. Go and enjoy yourselves.'

After Miriam and the lads had gone I took one of the reclining chairs outside, made myself comfortable with a beer, slipped off my shirt and opened Annan's notepad.

"Jim continued during dinner. ' There is no judgement. There is no judgement in the Universe. When a mountain cat kills a deer there is nothing that will decide whether it was right or wrong, or whether it was killed cleanly or in pain. When a flower blooms there is nothing that decides whether or not it is beautiful. Mankind is unique in nature, however. It is the only living thing that believes that it has the right to judge. It is part of its character. Men take on the role of Gods. So nothing is judging you apart from those people that you know, and yourself. The others have no power to change you, only to praise or rebuke. You, however, have the choice to make the changes that you need, and want to make, in order for you to be able to live in peace and fulfilment.

"You know, Annan, there are human vultures who like to sit on high rocks and watch victims die so that they can eat fully, despite having fat bellies. They are different to the vultures in nature that will wait for an injured or sick creature to die before they consume them in the process of purification and recycling. The human vultures will encourage the death of healthy individuals so that they can take pleasure from the destruction and carnage. They are parasites rather than cleaners. They are the lawyers, the ambulance chasers and the, so-called, claim-farmers.

"Some of the judicial judges become like that. They enjoy power for its own sake rather than for justice. The strange thing is that when things are done against good people with an intention of harm, very often those bad thoughts mature with time and then return to the giver. Maybe these people will only receive true justice at the hands of the Spirits when they move on and out of this land. I will ask for justice for you in my journey tonight.' Jim seemed more than a little bitter in his condemnation. I thought.

"Having listened intently, I explained to him that I believed spirits only lived in the minds of individuals as thoughts. There was no interconnection other than the flame of life itself and that was not a means of communication.

"Jim replied with an astute smile on his face. ' I totally agree with you. Yet I totally refute what you are saying!'

"After a while, he continued. ' Consider the Spirits to be the behaviours of people. Now imagine the other realities to be parts of their minds that influence those behaviours.

Those parts that influence are usually inaccessible. They are our emotions. We can feel them but we cannot find them as solid objects. In order to bring about change it is necessary to bring negative influences to the surface and then to replace them with positive and beneficial thoughts. Creating symbols and images can enable us to catch those feelings for a while. In this way we can change emotions such as hate to love, and sorrow to happiness. Look at the clouds for a moment. See! They are ever changing, ever moving and they are shapeless. It would be impossible to catch one and keep it. Yet when the cloud turns to rain, and the rain falls to the Earth, the cloud becomes water. Then the water can be caught and used. It can be kept safe."

Again, my professional approach was being shown in different cultural terms. Jung was a follower of the shamanic way and developed psychotherapy. He was a shaman in a suit. He managed to bring old ideas into a modern world. Fighting against the sexual drives of Freud, he sanitised shamanism for a sceptical world. I was eager for more. Rather than Annan lecturing, this was a real voice of change.

"Thoughts and dispositions for unacceptable behaviour are like clouds. If you can use a method to turn those thoughts into their equivalent of water, then you can deal with them. The negative emotions, like your anger for example, can become imaginary animals or monsters. To deal with them and destroy them, you use other symbols. For example, invent Protectors and Wise People. Then you feel that you are able to conquer the negatives. Those other things, your allies, are also emotions and feelings.

"So, on the one hand I can agree that there are not really other worlds in which strange creatures live other than in our own minds. But when we alter our behaviours then we alter the way we are. And when we do that we relate to others in a different way. So the change is internal but the way we communicate that change is external. When the cloud becomes water, the dirt in the water shows very easily. When the sun heats the water to make steam, the steam that rises is absolutely clean. The new cloud, the new thoughts have been purified.

"A wish is something which is a passive hope. When somebody makes a wish they don't really expect it to come true, but they have expressed a desire. There is no passion and no commitment to making that dream come to fruition because they have left it to some supernatural force to act on their behalf. As you know, the Spirits do not create the path of life for people. An ambition is different in that it involves the dreamer. It states an objective and adds the responsibility for its achievement.'

"I was not sure if I was more enlightened or more confused. I needed to process what had been said and to listen over and over to the recording."

I, on the other hand, was totally confused. I looked away from the words to attempt digestion. Then I became aware that Lillie had appeared from her van and I started to daydream that she would seduce me. My mind started to wander. It is true that men think of sex perpetually. She was a good looking girl and her body was like a statue, something to be admired even if it was not to be touched.

'Excuse me, Gee. Can I talk to you for a while?' Lillie was coyly standing in front of me.

'Be careful what you wish for, I thought. I looked at her. She was wearing a T-shirt and a pair of shorts.

I placed the notepad next to my beer. 'Of course you can.' I thought that she was going to invite us all for dinner and wanted to check our dietary habits. I wondered about the processes that had fulfilled my fantasy.

Lillie blushed as she started to talk.

'I saw Miriam and your sons disappear earlier. Adam is in Venice and I need some help with the cooker. Would you be kind enough to help, please?'

I stood up and followed Lillie into her trailer. It was a pretty place, neatly decorated with paintings of flowers. It was more like an apartment than a mobile home.

Lillie beckoned for me to sit down. I sank into the cushions as if submerging in a foam bath.

I had to say something, quickly. The situation made me uneasy. 'What is wrong with your stove?' My throat was dry and my words came out as a croak.

Without answering, she poured two glasses of wine, handed one to me and then sat down at a discreet distance from me. Then she said, 'It's a bit personal.' She talked in an intimate tone. 'You are a therapist, yeh?'

I nodded my agreement.

'Is everything you do truly confidential?'

I nodded again, wondering if her cooker needed psychotherapy. Perhaps it was really a delusional refrigerator.

'Adam is my brother. We are not lovers or boyfriends as people assume. I have a boyfriend but he is away at the moment and I need some company.'

Lillie reached to the back collar of her shirt and pulled it over her head in a single movement. It was a repeat of the first day on the beach. What I saw as Lillie sunbathed on the sand was then, theoretically prohibited. Now, she had taken the restriction away. She was showing me the things I had looked at illicitly. I felt the emotions of embarrassment and excitement collide in my mind.

I gulped loudly. Words of reproach were stuck in my throat. She stood up and slipped her shorts off. She flicked them into the air with her right foot and caught them in her hand. She threw them to the side and moved to me. I had an erection and she could see the bulge in my shorts.

I stared at her slim and naked body. The pubic hair, trimmed to a strip rather than a triangle, that I had briefly seen before on the beach was a focus for my gaze. This was my chance to savour this beautiful body standing before me, yet I was frightened.

I stood up and moved towards her.

'Lillie.' I almost whispered, not for effect but from nervousness.

She smiled back at me.

I fought the million year old hormonal development of mankind.

'Lillie. I am a married man. I cannot do anything. You are beautiful but I am unable to make love with you.' I backed off.

She moved to place her body in front of mine. She

touched my penis through the cloth of my shorts and I ejaculated. Embarrassed, I started to move to the doorway.

I looked at her and asked, 'What was that all about. You cannot be so desperate that you need the body of an old man.'

'That's why I wanted to talk to you. I'm an escort. A high class call-girl.' She blurted out. The last part was said almost with a sense of pride.

It was strange how that transition took place. As an innocent young woman she had been alluring, but as a hooker she instantly put herself into a different area of my mind. Perhaps thoughts of AIDS and other sexually transmitted diseases made her undesirable to me. Maybe it was the feeling of rejection of me as a person. She had been with a million other men and she only wanted me for money.

'Well I need some help. Can you help me? I'll pay you. I'll let you sleep with me if that is what you want.'

Now, at least she was looking for my professional services rather than selling hers.

'What help do you need?' I asked gingerly, edging to the door. I was puzzled by this sudden request. I was shocked that this beauty was within my grasp. My fantasy had become a bad experience.

'I want to lead a normal life. I want to escape from what I am and what I do.' She started to sob gently. Usually, in my office, I would reach for a tissue as quickly and adeptly as a wild western gun-slinger but I had none at hand.

'I don't see how I can, here. I would need to see you in my office.' I felt unable to help this girl.

'Let's start at the beginning. I've had counselling before, when I was sixteen, but all they asked me was how everything made me feel. That was silly because everything makes me feel like shit.'

I was confused and a little angry. 'You told me that you worked in a toy shop.'

'No. I said I sell pleasure products.' She pointed at her breasts and then her crotch. 'It is my way of avoiding telling people the truth about how I earn my living.'

'And Adam is a software engineer?'

'That is his way of saying that he is an escort for both

women and men. He makes soft things hard...if you get my drift, like I do.' She looked embarrassed as she pointed to my, now, lifeless member.

I nodded. In my years as a therapist I had been told nearly every sort of thing, but out of context hearing this information was a bizarre experience. I prepared to listen.

I asked her to dress.

Lillie pulled on her shorts and her shirt. Then she sat, saw it was her chance to talk and started. 'When I was a small girl I was abused by my father. When I was older, about ten, he shared me with his friends. They would come to the house, have some drinks and then take it in turns with me. That carried on until I was fifteen when I moved out and lived for a while with a man I had met. I had no qualifications having skipped school so I couldn't get a proper job. I then went to London where I met this bloke who looked after me. He said that we needed money. By that time I was on all sorts of drugs and they were expensive. They helped me to forget what had happened to me, the betrayal and everything.

I was, and am, an honest person so I refused to steal. As my body had given pleasure to men for years, it was not difficult to sell it rather than have it taken from me. That's when I tried the counselling to help me to come to terms with the way my life had turned out. That didn't seem to help so I carried on. I moved up the ladder, got myself a decent pimp who got me better work and that lasted for a couple of years. By then, I was making enough money to buy my own apartment and I got my clients by working the high-class clubs and casinos. Everything was good until I met this Indian bloke who threatened me with violence. He said that he'd smash my face and body if I didn't work for him. So I did. He makes money and so do I, but I live in fear everyday.'

'Where does Adam fit in?' I wanted the whole story.

'We met in a hotel room. There was this Arab who wanted to watch two people screwing. Sorry about the language...'

'It's OK' I said. 'Carry on.'

'So, to cut a long story short, we teamed up, not as

lovers, but like brother and sister. He's not my brother really, that's just part of our story. People get a kick out of watching what they think is incest. There are some sick bastards out there. Sorry, again. Anyway, we got new names and passports, opened up a Euro bank account, and bought our camper van. We have escaped.'

'So how can I help?' I was still baffled. Lillie had told me too much and I was not a policeman in the vice squad.

'I want you to get my memories out of my head. I want to become a woman who has no past. I want to be normal. We have money in the bank, but we have no happiness. I want Adam to become my man. He needs help as well. I want to find the thing that my father and his friends took. Self-respect, the ability to trust. Can you help me, Gee? Please. I'll do anything. I'll pay whatever it costs, I'll sleep with you if you want, but next time in a more romantic way…anything.'

Lillie crumbled into a small ball, sobbing, as if she had just been abused again. As she rolled up I could see her breasts under her shirt. Rather than being excited as I had before, I felt dirty, as if I had joined the vast ranks of men who had appropriated the essence of life from this unfortunate woman. This person who was offering her body to me to gain help to stop offering her body to other men.

Wondering what to do, I moved to obscure my view of the distraught figure.

'Helping you will take time, Lillie. If I could see you in my office after I get back from holiday, I am sure that I could resolve some of your issues, but I do not want to sleep with you.' Feeling lame, I had put a solution into the future. I had avoided becoming involved at that point of time.

'We have moved away from England. If we go back then Annan will kill us. He thinks he owns us.'

Everything stopped. The mention of Annan's name sent shivers down my spine. This was turning into a penny-thriller plot where coincidences are always contrived.

'Tell me about this man Annan.' Rather than being a request, I was asserting an order.

'As I said before, he is an Indian, quite old and seems charming on the outside but underneath he is a monster. He is known to have killed girls who have disobeyed him. He guards his girls and men like precious jewels.' She was spitting like a wild cat.

Annan's words came to my mind. The way to make money is by, "...discovering the needs of people and fulfilling them for profit." This was as bad as, "selling toys."

'Can you help me? Please. Can you help me?'

I had no answers that I could give her. A caravan in Italy was not a consulting room. It was inappropriate. As sorry for her as I felt, I was on holiday and that was nearly over.

'I do not think I can. Unless I can see you in proper surroundings then it is difficult for me. Why don't you contact the police? They would give you protection, I am sure.'

Without comment, Lillie stood up and asked me to leave. She glared at me, and with a look of hurt mixed with venom, said, 'You are like all of them, aren't you? I saw you looking at my tits the first day we came here. It was a free thrill for you. Now I'm asking for reimbursement, you have backed out. I'll get my own back. I'll tell your wife you raped me.'

Her words and tone erased the pitiable image of an abused child. Instead she a wrathful woman displacing the anger she felt towards her father, her other abusers and pimp onto me.

My holiday to relax and forget about the pressures of life and work had erupted like a fireball in my face. I returned to our caravan worrying about blackmail and the new face of Annan as a putrid and violent procurer of women. I went to the shower block where I washed and scrubbed myself and my shorts for at least half an hour. I dressed, returned to the van and collected my wallet. The appeal of Annan's words had been removed, but I picked up the notebook to take with me to the bar on the beach where I could drink and look for clues about this, now loathsome, man. How could his search for meaning in life be reconciled with the exploitation of people?

When I got there I missed out the reading and concentrated my efforts on drinking and smoking. Each cigarette reminded me of Lillie. Putting the tip into my mouth brought back Annan's words about nipples. Lewd thoughts made me imagine her nipples between my lips. That was enough to make me gag.

I had promised to cook dinner and I staggered back along the beach towards the shops. As I did, I half fell and half wobbled to sit on the sand.

'I'm sorry.' Lillie's voice was soft and childlike.

I turned to see this, now, innocent face smiling at me in a way that must have been used on countless men in the past. She sat next to me on the sand, pulled her knees to her chest and brushed her hair back with her hands. The black roots were showing through the blond colouring as she did so.

'I lied to you, Gee. I did not realise who you were. I was asked to check you out. That's what I did.'

I was mystified by her comment. Did she think that I was somebody else or had she been talking to someone about me? Lillie took off her T-shirt. To my relief, she was wearing a bikini top. I had no interest in a second round.

'I have to give you a message. When Annan arrives, he will explain everything to you. Stop fretting and start to enjoy the experience that you had. I know that I will always be in your memory bank from now on and for ever more. Let's make friends. I want you to look back on me with positive feelings.'

Lillie got up and walked away. I watched her. I was confused. She blew me a kiss as she faded into the distance.

When I returned to our caravan, Lillie and Adam had driven away. They were no more. I was both relieved and disappointed at the same time. I wondered about her last comment until the point when Miriam came back with a pair of smiling lads wearing new clothes and with new hairstyles. Miriam did not even notice that our neighbours had gone until after she had cooked dinner. She remembered that we had been invited for drinks but our hosts had flown the nest.

'Probably to do with the screaming we heard. I bet she was coming onto somebody and he got jealous.' Miriam had the solution. She also knew that I was a little drunk and seemed slightly depressed.

We went for a walk before going to bed. Miriam gazed at the full moon. 'Look, Gee. The moon is pulling a face of shock. It is as if it is making an "oooh" sound. I wonder what it has seen today to make it look so surprised. What were you up to while we were shopping?'

Her giggle defused the moment seconds before I had a new panic attack.

CHAPTER ELEVEN

THE MOON'S TEARS

thursday

All-in-all, on balance, the plants were nice things, but strange, for the reasons stated before. But, even they were not immune to outside forces. Some of the aliens ate them. Sometimes the Hand-of-God would pull them out of the world. If, and when, they came back, they usually had received some brutal surgery. The fish were horrified when the grass-snake slid into the pond for the first time. It started to consume the fish one by one.

We were going to Venice for the second time. I took Annan's notes with me. I wanted more information about this horrible man who I thought should be reported to the police when we got home. As I sat on the ferry, the words in Annan's book seemed to strike a chord of relevance.

"I needed to ask Jim about judgement. I wanted to know why my wife had left me. 'So, please tell me why, if there is Great Universal Spirit, does it allow bad things to happen? If the universe lives in all things then why doesn't it change the wrongdoing? Why does it need to torture us? It seems that the good men are punished for being good. Those who work, give and share, end up losing what they love the most. Those who are idle, those who take and hold are the ones who seem to have happy lives. It is not enough to say that there is no appraisal. There is assessment on Earth. Others judge the individual, and the individual judges himself. If the Spirit of the Universe lives in all things, then the Universe has an opinion of our worth. If we live in the Spirit of life, then surely we can be allowed to enjoy the Spirit of happiness and fulfilment before we go to meet our maker.'

"I did not feel annoyed, but frustrated. My words were more a plea for man, animal and plant kind. I was answering the claim of being non-judgmental with an evaluation of the Great Spirit based on my own experiences.

"Then I started to feel angry. I thought that I had the right to feel this way because I was now defending those people that I loved. I was annoyed that their lives, as well as mine, had been so badly affected by this amorphous thing that was at the base of all life, at the root of all things.

"Jim had not responded, so I continued. ' And now I will reply to what you asked when I got here. I want the truth about the Universe. I want to know if it really is worth saving. You said that this is a place where I can fulfil what I want! Well, I want to accomplish my duty as a good husband and a father, and a grandfather in time. I want to replace the misery that I gave my loved-ones with happiness. So grant me that.'

"Jim answered after a pause. ' Have you finished? I will assume so.' His tone was neither dismissive, nor sarcastic. It was, however, firm. 'What you had in your life was choice. That is freedom. You had the choice to carry hurt into the lives of others. Who do you want to blame for the options you had? Do you want to be so controlled that you run your life as a stream does when contained by its banks? Or would you prefer to have the freedom of an ocean.

"What is really getting to you, Annan, is that whereas you had the ability to decide how you would behave, you did not improve until you had to. And now that you have changed, you're upset because your wife had that freedom of choice about whether to take you back or to throw you away. You have learnt many things, but you have still not learnt to overcome your own disappointment in not being able to make people do as you desire.

"The Great Spirit of life is not a wishing well. If it were, then all beings could be as selfish as they wanted to be, as nasty as suited them, and then they could ask for forgiveness. Everything would be without a conscience. As you said, there are people who are knowingly selfish and who steal both emotional and material belongings from others. They have the choice to change as you did with your anger.'

"'But,' I replied, 'what stops them from doing that? Are they ever punished if they are not judged?'

"Jim answered quickly. ' Yes. They are punished by

themselves because they never have what they want. If they have to take or hurt, then that is something that they feel they have to do. If they feel that they have to take something, then it is because they are suffering without it. Of course, once they have got something, then they will need something else, and so on. In that way they are never happy. The people who are happy are the ones who give freely, and without conditions, something that they want to supply to make others happy. In that way happiness breeds happiness. And misery breeds misery. And you have learnt that at first hand.'

"I was shocked. ' So if I had been able to stop giving anger and the fear that caused, and had given pure love instead, we would all have been happy.'

"I waited in silence for a long while. ' Is it too late now? Will I ever get the chance to give the love that I feel, but which had been obscured by the anger that has now been tamed?'

"Jim seemed to be working on the words that he would deliver, and after a long while started to explain. ' Annan, there are four elements; the air, the wind, the Earth and water. There are four directions; the north, the east, the south and the west.

"There are four forms of life. The animals, the plants, the elements of the rocks and Earth, and of course, the Spirits. What you need to know now is that there are also four worlds."

I had read enough. The many facets of the man were beating at each other like rocks falling in an avalanche. The prostitute he held by threat and who he had persuaded to deny what she had told me. The wife who he had sent away with his anger. The kind man who wanted to help me to stop smoking. The man who was seeking relief with a shaman, probably engulfed in a psycho-active trance entered with cactus juice. It was too much. Around Annan there was chaos, hurt and destruction. That much, at least, summed up life.

The book broke as it hit the seat. The anger contained in its notes seemed to add force to my throw.

'Why did you do that?' Miriam demanded rather than asked.

'Because the man is a lunatic. He is nasty.' I ended the conversation.

Soon after my flash of anger, the ferry docked close to St Marks Square. This visit to Venice was to discover a city that had been made unavailable by my panic a few days before. I had been given orders that it would be fun.

'Isn't that Adam?' Miriam queried.

'I shouldn't think so.' I replied. 'Venice is too New Testament to have Adam and Eve in it.' I was serious.

'No. Adam from the campsite.' Miriam pointed. 'Yes and that's his floozy with him, what's-her-name? Lillie.'

I had noticed that Miriam did that. She pretended to forget the names of anybody she thought might be competition, even for an old man like me.

Lillie and Adam were walking along like two tourists seeing the city for the first time. I stopped to adjust my footwear in order to prevent any attempts to catch their attention, or to be recognised. When I had finished they were out of sight.

'So where are we going?' I asked. We had been told by Walter Evans that the best way to explore Venice was to get lost. And so we did.

We all felt hungry after walking for miles through narrow alleys and climbing bridges. We needed food, so for lunch we found a small café well off the beaten track. They are supposed to be cheaper.

'What is the local speciality?' I asked a young man behind the counter.

'Polenta.' He replied

'What's that made from?' I wanted to know more. I had heard of the dish, but I had no idea what it was.

'Mice.'

'What? Mice?' My hands mimed the running of a mouse through the air.

'No. Mize. You call eet sweetcorn.'

'Ah! Maize.' The laughter from Miriam and the lads increased my embarrassment.

'I'll have the risotto, please.' I needed to distance myself from the local speciality.

We wandered around in an attempt to help us to digest our lunches and we visited the usual attractions. Harry's Bar, the opposite to a church Then the Jewish quarter that was reminiscent of the black and white footage of ghettos in the days of Hitler. There seemed to be no humour there, only sad reminiscence.

Venice is a beautiful city that is beyond my capacity to describe fully. I was more aware of the feelings of its dwellers over centuries of hedonism, bloodshed and death.

In the main shopping areas the rivals for the powers of the churches were abundant. Fashion stores selling brand names rather than clothing. Models smiled from the advertising photographs in the windows seducing customers to adopt the same body shapes as the anorexics I had treated. Fast food stores were enticing the opposite effect of large portions for small amounts of money. The international corporations were holding their collection plates out for payment for the promise of eternal beauty or for feasting on the fatted lamb-burger. The world seemed to be everywhere. That is, the world designed and owned by mankind.

To pass time on the ferry back to the caravan park I started to read again. I had the motivation of a detective looking for clues. I was not even aware which crime had been committed. Annan was a user of women for gain against a background of violence and threat.

"The four worlds are defined by time. There is the here-and-now. Think carefully and you will see a reflection of yourself as you are; confused, questioning and lost.

'Then there is the past. You will see the anger that you had. You can see its defeat. Visiting the past is about the retrieval of those things which need to be dealt with.

'Once those negatives have been retrieved then the reconciliation of those lost parts of your mind is achievable. The extinction of your anger takes place and you are able to be at peace with yourself and others. The next world is where constructive advice is taken to leave the past and to change the present to make a different future. The fourth world is where choices are made available. One thing that you should take to heart is that you are responsible for your own destiny. Conceive your fate and it will happen. I will show you."

This was a weird and wonderful version of my job. I deal with resolving issues in the pasts of my clients to enable them to look to the future. However, I am free of the strange spiritual linguistics that the medicine man was using. I carried on reading.

"Jim sounded different, as if he were speaking the words of someone else, the collective voice of the four faces.

"He asked me to imagine that I was looking into the fourth world where I could see how in those earlier times, after I had quarrelled with my wife, I had started to think that my marriage was going to end. That belief widened the gap that started to grow between us. And after the next, and the next, and the next arguments, the gap became a valley, which then became a canyon.

"'Can you see that what has happened is what you saw your destiny to be? And the actions that you took, allowing your anger to surface, just brought that destiny to reality?'

"I remember nodding my sad agreement. I looked at Jim and noticed that he was smiling. 'Why are you smiling at my downfall?' I asked, feeling very irritated.

"'Because what you are watching is not only your downfall, but it is also your salvation. Can't you see? You now have the answer to your persistent question. How you can change somebody else for your own benefit? This is the revelation that you wanted. If you caused your situation by your vision of the end, then you can change your life by assuming it to be the way you want it to be. If you really want to live your days out with somebody in harmony, happiness, security and love, then all you have to do is believe that outcome will happen, and no other. That is why I am smiling. When you dream your dream, then your dream will come true.

"'We have all met people who have become ill because they think that they will succumb to sickness. There are also people who have lots of things because they think that they deserve them. The key thing to know is that we get what we think we will. We all control our own destinies. We shape our own lives. Who else would want to write scenarios for every living thing? Do you think that Spirits have nothing better to do? We are not handed a script at birth. Life is a play that we write ourselves.

"'We are all part of the Universe so what we want is what the Universe gives us. Regard the Universe as a container of all of the support that we need. The props for the play are available. All we have to do is to ask for those resources. Fate is the thing that seems to move you in the direction of fulfilling those dreams. It is the vehicle for its delivery.'

"I asked Jim if he could tell the future. I wanted to know what would happen in my life.

"He told me that the fortune tellers who sell their skills are of two types. Those who guess what you want to hear and then sell the good news to you. Then there are those who know what you want, and then help you to put into operation all of those things that are needed to achieve it. The second group is very rare because they are the ones who understand how the Universe works.

"It seems strange, but when you are pledged to achieving your dreams, then things appear to you in an extraordinary way. You find coincidences, signs and omens. Helpful people seem to appear from nowhere. You find help from the most unusual sources. The only thing that you have to do is believe, not in an outcome that is preordained, but in your access, by right, to your share of the tools and assets of the Universe that will make your dreams come true.

"I think that should be stated in even stronger terms. Know what you want to happen, and the appearance of the resources that are needed to bring that about, will take place, almost spontaneously. You are the one who creates that which will come to be. Hey! You met me, didn't you?'

"I burst out laughing, not in ridicule but in relief. 'But isn't that using power for my benefit? What if my wife's dream is different to mine?' I asked.

"He was forthright. 'Then there will be two outcomes. The one she wants in her life and the one you want in yours. The lives you have will still happen, they do not have to be the same. I think you have seen enough to know that life is not predestined or straightforward.

"If we can live in these four realities simultaneously then we can live the lives that we choose rather than the ones that we fear we will live. You have great examples of this already. When you first saw your wife you dreamed that this beautiful girl would one day be your wife. When you married you knew that you would have children who you would be proud of. All of those positive things happened.

"If you want to live the rest of your life with somebody who loves you and then rebuild that dream, believe it will happen, and then the world of Fate and Destiny will ensure that it will.

"See and feel your dreams as new experiences rather than remembering your past. Only memories are from the past. You need to create a new future with new events. But perhaps your destiny lies with somebody else. Never disregard that possibility.'

"I asked Jim, 'Who are you?'. I felt as if Jim was more than he appeared."

That was the same question I had asked Annan and the same feeling, I thought to myself before returning to the notepad.

"He replied with a smile. 'I am a part of the Universe like you and everything else. I am nothing special. I have no more rights than a grain of sand in this desert.'

"I continued. 'But you know more than most.' 'These worlds aren't real, are they?'

"His tone was becoming tired. 'Find out for yourself. Use what you have heard to bring about transformations for the world.'

"I asked Jim my final question. 'Should my aim become that of making changes to the people who would save the planet, not my marriage? That would be too selfish, only caring for myself, wouldn't it?' Jim smiled his concurrence and hugged me gently. I never saw him again."

Underneath the notes there was a little drawing of a Red

Indian war bonnet on an old man's head. I wondered if this was a sketch of Jim.

I had read enough. This man, a user of women for prostitution and profit had decided to save the planet.

'If I ever see Annan again, I will punch him.' My words alarmed Miriam.

'What is the matter? What have you found in the book?'

Resisting the temptation to throw the notepad into the sea, I rammed it towards Miriam. 'Read it for yourself. He's a pimp.'

She put it into her bag for safekeeping.

I looked up at the moon. All I could see was a face with a tear running from its left eye.

Moments after, I realised that there was nothing about prostitutes in Annan's writing.

CHAPTER TWELVE

BODIES OF CHANGE

Friday

The fish wanted life to be easier. They wanted to have more room to swim. They wanted less danger. They wanted more food. Even though they should have been happy, they felt that life had more to offer. They felt that their God should be more benevolent. The man that the fish thought was a God sat in a garden chair next to his pond. He watched the fish slowly swimming around. The man was drinking a beer with his friend. They were discussing life and death, as men do when inspired to philosophy by alcohol.

'What was your outburst about last night, Gee?' Miriam had flicked through the parts of Annan's notes that she had not read before. 'I got up early this morning and I didn't see anything about whores.'
I was saved from further interrogation by the arrival of Walter Evans. He threw his bicycle down, as usual, and wobbled over to inspect our plate of croissants.
I nodded my invitation for him to help himself.
'Were you talking about the prostitutes that have plied their trade in Venice for centuries?'
In order to avoid talking about Annan directly, I concurred with his conclusion.
He decided to prove his faith by referring to the words of the New Testament. He took a copy of the Bible from his pocket, telling us that it was his First Aid kit for sinners, flicked through the pages and started to read aloud.

"Do you not know that he who unites himself with a prostitute is one with her in body? For it is said, 'The two will become one flesh.' But he who unites himself with the Lord is one with him in spirit. Flee from sexual immorality. All other sins a man commits are outside his body, but he who sins sexually sins against his own body. Do you not know that your body is a temple of the Holy Spirit, who is in you, whom you have received from God? You are not your own, you were bought at a price. Therefore honour God with your body."

We were silent.
'Corinthians.' Walter gave the source.
He continued. 'I wanted to tell you more about the Holy Spirit, and I found this quote yesterday. I love coincidences. They are the hints we get from the Lord.'
We remained silent. I was worried that Miriam was beginning to suspect something. She was beginning to worry about me.
'The reason I popped by is to say 'goodbye.' We are driving home later and I wanted to thank you for coming to my service last Sunday.' He gestured that he would like another croissant. We gestured back that he should eat more as Miriam and I had lost our appetites.
Walter wiped the crumbs from his mouth, shook hands with us and mounted his cycle. He wobbled away to find more food at the caravans of the other members of his small parish as we cleaned the grease, transferred from Walter's hand to our palms, on our shorts, like children.
Miriam glared at me.
'So what is this stuff about prostitutes and Annan? Have you two been out on the town? You told me that you were chatting the other night. Perhaps you were doing more than that.'
'I told him about one of my clients.' I lied.
'Why did you call him a pimp? Pimps procure girls for men and take their money. There was nothing about Annan being a user of women. Tell the truth, Gee.'
My choice was straightforward. Fight or flight. I could attack Miriam's words or I could run. I chose to walk away, the very action that would show that I was hiding a truth.
The holiday I had looked forward to so much had turned into a horror. I had not made love with Lillie, but my conscience told me that I had. I was carrying a guilt that I had no ownership of. I was unable to explain the events of the day before yesterday to Miriam. She would not believe that I had turned down the chance to have sex with a

beautiful young woman. The trap was that I would have to explain that to her before I could tell her the truth about the man she had come to admire.

As I entered the coffee shop in the main square, I heard a noise that I sent a shudder through my body.

'Hello, Gee. How are you this fine morning?' Annan was standing in front of me.

I said to him, 'Where is your fucking morality? You are nothing more than a pimp. You use young people to make money for yourself. You are a bastard. All this New Age do-gooder stuff is bullshit that stains and smells.' I started to walk away, sneering.

Annan shouted after me. So you want to know my secrets. You want to know what I am all about. Well, listen.'

I sat down on a bench, my heart pumping as if I was about to punch this piece of sewage. Yet, I wanted to hear what this piece of low-life had to say. I needed validation of my intense hatred.

'After my wife and I were divorced, I became more and more interested in the spiritual life that was being dissolved and eroded in the older parts of the world. I guess you have read my account of my visit to see Jim, the Native American Indian. He primed my mind to search for a way to help the planet to recover from the devastation that is going on. By-the-way, I left my notes for you to read. I was going to give them to you but forgot in the disruption caused by a very personal phone-call.

'Anyway, my idea was born after I visited Africa to talk to the witch-doctors, as they are disparagingly called. I saw people getting rich and people starving in so many parts of that wonderful continent. It hurt me to stay in hotels where the poor were serving the wealthy. One evening after visiting a settlement for the Kalahari Bushmen, I was writing up some notes about how the oldest culture in the world was being corralled out of their habitat for the sake of mineral and plant rights. I went to the bar where I was approached by a South African woman. At first I thought she was another tourist but she, with great charm, played her hand. She was a hooker. We talked about why she had turned to the oldest profession and she said that she had lost every penny when apartheid had ended. I didn't want to have her, but I paid her fee for conversation rather than for lovemaking. She seemed relieved. Perhaps I was not that desirable. She told me that slept with men who seemed to be affluent because they were above admitting that they needed casual sex to build edifices on their, already gigantic, egos.

'We drank and talked more. She took me to her room. She refused to come to mine. She undressed and started to undress me. Sorry, but this is all a bit embarrassing. She asked me for more money…anyway, we got into bed and had sex. She was good at the theatrical parts of making me feel that I was the greatest lover in the world, the opposite of how my wife had described me.

'After our romping, we continued to chat. Jessie, a fake name I guessed, said that she needed money to feed her two children. Her husband had been killed in a riot and her world had collapsed. She took from the rich to give to her poor offspring.

'We talked and made love over three days. By then it was making love rather than having sex. The foundation of our relationship changed from what she could do for me for money to what we could do to redistribute wealth to those in need. We wanted to steal from the pharmaceutical companies who put profits before affordable prices. She knew people whom had lost their children to AIDS and malaria for the want of cheaper drugs. We wanted to influence the destinations for arms and ammunition. Politicians encourage instability so that other countries do not become competitors. Instead, they become consumers of weapons. We wanted to sway the minds of politicians who were involved in wars and the stripping of the assets of countries and the resources of the planet.

'In other words we wanted to bring about a global transformation by changing the minds of the men who used obscene power to bring about chaos, death and destruction. We wanted to encourage peace and sharing. The last part in my notebook explains why my visit with Jim had set me up to do something constructive, but I did not know what to do until I met Jessie.

I remember her saying, "Those cock-suckers are ruining

the heritage of our innocent children. Let the real cocksuckers stop them."

'That was the inspiration. Robin Hood stole from the rich to give to the poor by using his bow and arrows. We would use the arrows of men to bring about their downfalls. Their cocks would crow our tune.'

Annan's face showed a mixture of pride and embarrassment at his rhetoric.

'Jessie was good. She showed me the hidden microphones and cameras in her room. That is why she had refused to come to my room in the hotel. She told me that photographs and tape recordings enabled her to follow up her clients. Men would boast about company mergers and take-overs. Politicians would talk about what they were planning. Her profits would be invested in shares. Her money was laundered in a way that was legitimate.

'We had a harmony that was unique. It was almost like a confession of her past blended with subtle boasting about her initiative.

'Rather than spending more time with the local shamans, we plotted an expansion of Jessie's business that would prevent her from having to work on her back. Anyway, I felt jealous at that prospect.

'To cut a long story short, we moved to London with her children and started building a business. We recruited women and, when we understood more about people such as politicians, business leaders, pop-stars, actors and churchmen; we added men to please them. We discovered their weaknesses, set up long term relationships, learned about their plans and actions and then used the information to invest, change minds or exhort money. The money, by the way, was used to finance the recording equipment we needed in the short-term, but its main use was to help the people in the, so-called, Third World.

None of our staff has been coerced into doing what they do. They are all willing volunteers who can see a bigger picture. They enjoy the feeling of contribution they make to stopping wars, bloodshed and civil murder by neglect. In Hollywood it is acceptable to lie on the casting couch for well paid parts. Nobody compels them. They do it for gain, but nobody ever calls them whores.

If one man had gone against the code of not killing and had put a bullet through Hitler's head, should he be deemed a murderer for saving the lives of millions of people? If a willing woman commits her body to the pleasures of a politician who can then be persuaded to invest in areas of poverty to prevent thousands of eight and nine and ten year old girls from having to sell their bodies for a few coins and the HIV virus, should she be called a whore or a saint?

'Where is my morality, you asked? It is slightly above that of our customers.

'Organisations rule the world by using threats, power and violence. Make love, not war, Gee. Screw the money and influence out of the powerful and give it to their victims. We are like a bunch of angels, not devils. The men and women do it because they have a belief in the principles of a universal sharing. We all want revenge on abusers of all kinds from the paternal to the corporate.'

Annan had made a long speech and I needed time to absorb it. I resisted the temptation to be judgmental. I wondered if he had a real justification.

'What about Lillie?' I needed to know.

'Let's get a coffee.' Annan walked to the coffee shop. I followed.

After we had ordered and received our drinks, Annan looked at me with that expression that I had learnt signalled another long dissertation.

'Sorry, Gee.' He stopped.

After a while I indicated that I wanted more.

'You were set up. I wanted to test your morality. As I have told you before, you stopped my daughter from committing suicide many years ago. From what she told me at the time I knew that you were a man of great integrity. After I met you on the plane and realised who you are, I wanted to recruit you to continue the business for me. I am getting old and I want to retire. I want to search for my daughter in India. My problem is that I cannot find anybody who I trust enough to help me out. My sons run other businesses that are fair-trade companies. I cannot involve them in this. They know nothing about what I do. They think I am an eccentric old man who enjoys travelling.

'After I met you on the plane, I called some people who I knew could influence things. I booked the hotel here and purposely bumped into you and your family. You seemed to want to understand the difference between the life on the planet and those people of power who want to exploit it. You have empathy. Lillie was sent to temp you. She was the apple in Eden. If you had tried to taste the fruit then you would not be the man that I think you are. A man could not help in a business like mine if he cannot resist sampling the goods for sale.

'Anyway, I have decided not to recruit you after all. I am not sure that the scheme fits your sense of morality. I think that you would find it too difficult to reconcile the two poles of virtue.'

Annan called the waitress and paid her.

'It was good meeting you, Gee. Perhaps we will meet again, one day.'

He left before I could reply.

'Would you like another coffee?' I turned, expecting to see the waitress. It was Miriam. She sat down and indicated that we wanted drinks.

'That was Annan, wasn't it? Are you ready to tell me what is going on?'

I told her what had been said, omitting any mention of Lillie. Miriam's attention was intense.

'I like the idea.' Why don't you consider it?'

I was surprised at my wife's reaction. She had a higher sense of right and wrong than I did. The concept should have appalled her.

I had to tell her that I was not being considered for the job anymore.

'Go after him. He'll be at the hotel. Ask him what he is looking for.'

I was tempted, but refused to seek out the old man. We returned to our van, woke the lads and went to the beach.

CHAPTER THIRTEEN

THE ASS OF THE LAW

Saturday

"It is difficult to accept that there is a God." The man said. "Whenever I pray for something that I need, my prayers never seem to be answered. If God existed, surely He would provide everything that I need for a happy life. My car needs upgrading. I want to build a swimming pool. Why can't He let me have the money I need?"
He opened another bottle and sighed. "Look at the easy life the fish in my pond have. All of their needs are taken care of and they never thank me for what I do. They don't realise how easy their lives are."

After Annan's departure and my explanations, peace finally arrived in our rented Eden. We had slept well and had woken with a sense of making the most of our last couple of days.

New neighbours had arrived early in the morning. When we returned with our breakfast, an Englishman greeted us with a sense of formality and salesmanship.

'Hello, my name is Roger Wilson. This is my good lady, Suzie. We are from Surrey. This is my card. I am a lawyer. Holidays are stressful, but if you need to buy a property, divorce your wife or write a will, my firm can help.' With a small laugh, a flick of his head and a shake of his hand he returned to his very grand camper van. Suzie waved 'hello' with her smile and joined him.

Stifling a belly laugh, I looked at Miriam. She was containing her giggles.

'Roger is a great name for a brief. Roger and Sue. I bet they are the main partners.' Miriam was unable to stop laughing out loud.

'Screw them and Sue-do.' I added, without a smile.

I had always had a cynical view of lawyers and the law. It seemed to me that the law was about profit rather than justice. The whole system is made so difficult to comprehend that it enables lawyers to charge huge fees to understand the language on everybody else's behalf. Justice should be a simple thing about hurt and right and wrong. I had seen victims whose abusers had gone unpunished because they could afford barristers who could make deft twists and turns with detail and language. I wondered if they would use the same craft to liberate the man who had harmed their own eight year old daughters.

As if reading my thoughts, Miriam chipped in. 'Why do lawyers have to charge VAT on divorces? Value Added Tax! What value do they add to one of the most stressful things that people can go through? And talking of stress, how about death and moving house. They charge for living and dying. Plus VAT, of course.'

Miriam had been sexually harassed by a lawyer in one of her jobs. She was forced to leave after she was told by an independent law firm how much it would cost to pursue her claim against him.

This would be our last full day in our camp. We had adjusted to the claustrophobia and the climate, but it was time to go home. Annan had left, the boys were bored and I was more stressed than before we came. This had been not so much an adventure but more a journey into chaos. It had been not so much a break from routine as an intensive exercise in self analysis. My moral fibre had been stretched and woven into a straightjacket that was impossible to escape from.

We decided to pack in the evening, ready for our departure on Sunday morning. Miriam wanted to go into the town on her own to do some last minute shopping for gifts for her parents. My feeling was that she wanted to be without company for at least part of one day. The lads and I agreed to lounge around on the beach. At least with my sons there I would not be exposed to temptation.

While the young men kicked a ball around, I took my last view of non-familiar naked flesh. Unexcited, I read a newspaper that I had bought with a pack of cigarettes on our way to our resting place. Another celebrity had signed a book-writing contract that would tell a hungry audience how she had found fame along with her breast implants. Another politician had been caught with a call-girl. Another priest had been caught with a choir boy. Another bank had announced record profits. Agreements on carbon dioxide emissions were not being fulfilled. There was one article that talked about the balance of wealth.

"If the Chinese are perceived to be lower beings than Westerners then we can tolerate their poor and unhealthy working conditions to cheapen the cost of goods for a better lifestyle for us. Slavery and general abuse continue but it is sprayed with a perfume that makes it smell sweeter than it did two hundred years ago. Yet, this is now a world where the ugly are made desirable by testing cosmetics and fragrances on beautiful animals so that the beautiful are maimed in producing products that can only disguise and cover up the rancour that is at the base of human kind."

Nothing was new in the news. Greed, exploitation and abuse made headlines, but the disclosure made no difference.
The crossword made me cross and the cartoons were not funny. I think I was a bit depressed.
'Lighten up, dad. You look as if you are about to cry.' Mark's voice brought some warmth to the sunshine.
As I joined in kicking the ball, I wondered if Annan had anything to do with the exposure of the politician. That well respected representative of voters had been, after all, caught conducting an arms deal with rebel forces who were doing their best to kill British peace keeping troops.
We lunched together with a café pizza. Miriam had not returned and I was too lethargic to attempt cooking, even though we had the collection of edible spare parts that build up on a self-catering holiday.
Back on the beach, I sat and pondered. I wondered if my experiences had changed my view of life.
I found that my connection to the Universe was like trying to open a combination lock or solving a riddle while standing next to a door that is already open. The mind talks to the soul that in turn might talk to the Universe. I was unable to make the leap from my natural cynicism to

spirituality. I needed proof. I wanted that whisper from the Universe to be louder.

In the past I had seen drunks in parks mumbling at passers-by. I had wondered if they had found the answer to life through their indulgence in alcohol, but had paid a price of secrecy. They might know the solution but nobody could understand their denouement as they were always incoherent. But at least they tried to share their secrets, unlike the pyramids of power.

I felt the same way as when listening to the drunks. Somebody was nudging me, somebody was trying to tell me something, but I was unable to hear the message. My ears were unable to hear because they were intoxicated by the onslaught of too many messages that I was unable to comprehend.

Late in the afternoon we wandered back to our caravan. We said goodbye to the beach as if it were a person. I stood and gazed at the sandscape, a word I had invented a few days before, and then slowly walked away.

As we arrived, Miriam was wobbling down the track. She had been drinking, that was obvious. She must have stopped for lunch and drunk more than was within her capacity.

She only had a few small bags with her, so she had spent more time consuming than buying.

'Hello, Gee. Hello boys.' She slurred her way past us into the van, where she fell asleep.

I gave Mark some money and sent him to get some spit-roasted chickens for our supper. Miriam emerged and sat at the table in silence. She looked glum.

'Are you alright?' I asked.

'Fan-bloody-tastic.' She closed her eyes and asked for a glass of wine.

I poured a very small one for her. She was a different person to the woman I knew. She had changed, somehow.

'Is there something wrong? You seem...'

'I seem, what?' Her tone was aggressive.

As if scenting the blood of disharmony in the air as a shark detects blood, Roger and Sue arrived with a bottle of champagne.

'We have found a place to buy. We would like you to celebrate with us. Nobody else around here seems to speak English. Trouble with Italy. Too many foreigners, ha, ha!'

Without any response from us, Roger deftly opened the bottles. 'We need some glasses, old boy. Don't suppose you have champers glasses. Susie, darling, get some from our place.'

The boys escaped. 'We're off to the beach.' They called as they ran.

Roger and Sue sat down. 'Bit of good luck, today. We found a place along the coast. Bloody massive and I screwed a good price. We are travelling through Europe in search of a couple of getaway retreats. Made a lot of money from claims on the tsunami way back and it's time to shove it into property.'

He did not know our names and he was bragging. He needed people with less money than himself to wave his wealth at.

Susie returned with cut glass champagne flutes and Roger poured.

'Cheers. Hey we don't even know your names.' Without waiting for them he took a swig from his glass, made noises of appreciation of his own taste in purchasing the best, and continued.

'I'm not the sort of lawyer who handles house sales and divorces. I chase natural disasters like earthquakes and floods. The things that folk call Acts of God. Well if God causes them, somebody has to clean up, and that's what I do. I clean up. And that's how I make piles of money. Disaster is always double-sided. If somebody loses, then I make sure I win. Governments don't want to pay out compensation, so they hire me to beat off claims. I work out to be slightly cheaper. Every time there is a flood or earthquake, my bank manager wants to buy me lunch. Bloody good bloke.' Roger laughed.

'Well, fuck you.' Miriam had opened her eyes at last. She swigged her champagne in one go.

'I beg your pardon.' Roger seemed shocked. 'There is at least one lady present.' He pointed at Susie.

'I suggest you go.' I spat at Roger.

'Perhaps that's best. She will throw up at any minute, I reckon.'

'So will I.' I replied. 'Now piss off.' Even in that moment of anger I managed to omit saying, 'you bastard', in case he tried to sue me for defamation.

Grabbing their precious glassware from our hands, they stormed away. 'I'll get you, you little pipsqueak.' Roger threatened.

Miriam and I burst out laughing and then fell silent once again.

Mumbling angry sounds, Miriam was falling asleep. The champagne was something that would have better avoided. My mind wandered around Roger and his parasitic nature.

I spoke to myself, softly, as if talking to Annan. 'People are like cells in a body. The DNA in each cell can duplicate the whole body, yet each cell is an individual. When they go wrong, they are like a cancer that can destroy the whole. The cure is to cut it out before everything dies. The Universe is like the body. People can kill it because they are greedy and malevolent. The individual is a cell in the Universe that contains everything and should help the whole to be healthy. Yet when individuals become greedy and malevolent, then they have the potential to destroy everything.'

I caught a glimpse of myself in one of the windows. 'Shit! I'm turning into Annan.' I said to my mirror image.

I wondered why Miriam had gone out and got drunk. It was most unlike her. I wanted to ask her but she was fast asleep and, for my safety, I would let her rest. I did the packing myself as best as I could. The lads would have to stuff their clothes into their bags when they returned from the beach, and Miriam would have to find somewhere for her clothes. I wanted to escape but I could not leave Miriam on her own in the caravan.

The only option was to sit quietly in the open air and wait for something to happen. I was worried that I would start to think back over the last two weeks. This Eden had sprung ambushes. Annan had set my mind racing at a time when it should have been quiet. The boys had experienced their most unexciting holiday and Miriam and I appeared to be at different places in our marriage.

I started to bring parallel lines to a point. If this place was Eden, then who were Adam and Eve? Was Annan the God figure and the Lillie the temptation of the serpent? If she were, then why had I refused to eat the apple? Certainly, the metaphor of the creation of man in the Bible had seemed clear. Knowledge is a dangerous thing. Or is it? Certainly carnal knowledge would have been. Yet knowledge for improvements for every inhabitant of the planet is to be sought. The abuse of knowledge for selfish gain is to be abhorred. That gives a higher rung on the ladder that enables people to look down on others. People like Roger.

I wondered at which point a group is formed. Two or more men? Then I wondered when a tribe is created. Then a country, a nation, an alliance of nations. The common factor is the grouping together for personal benefit. Yet, it was unclear when it goes wrong because when nations are at war they are attacking for greed, or defending to protect what they have. However, when nations are sent to war in order to benefit a few at the top of the hierarchy at the expense of the lives of young soldiers, everybody but a few will lose.

The idea that man was tempted, or rather a woman was, is strange. Why did God allow it to happen? Was the system imperfect at the beginning? Or was it to see how imperfect mankind is? If God was created by men in the image of himself, then the blame could be attributed elsewhere, the thing we have done for ever. My lot is not good enough. Blame the blacks, the Jews, the Muslims, the Catholics, the Protestants...everybody who is not like me. Women, of course! Let's blame them. Eve was a woman after all.

As if to defend against what I was thinking, Miriam shouted from the caravan.

'Gee. Come here, please.'

I went into the caravan where Miriam was filling a bucket with vomit. After ensuring that she was safe and being told to leave her alone, I went outside.

The boys were returning. They ran up the pathway, full of life. I smiled at them and walked towards the bars. Miriam could explain her predicament to her sons, herself.

CHAPTER FOURTEEN

WHO'S FAULT?

Sunday

The other man replied. "Sometimes I think that our understanding of our Creator is like those fish think of you. They can theorise and speculate all they want, but they will never comprehend what really happens in the world outside the pond that they think is their world. How sad it must be to be so restricted in their thinking." He paused. "Let's have another beer."

I was looking forward to going home. The holiday, Holy Day had not been days of rest. They had been stressful, thought provoking and challenging in a negative way. Miriam had a hang-over and the lads were grumpy because I had insisted that they packed their own bags. I was just bloody miserable.

We cleaned the caravan, put things where we had found them, locked up and strolled to the check-out point. I paid the bill and we left the Garden of Eden. I was not sorry to go. As we walked to the bus stop it was a release rather than an expulsion.

Miriam was quiet. I knew that there would be many words that would be spoken at some point in the future. For a start, I wanted to know why she had drunk so much on the day before. The journey to the airport was the mirror image of our arrival, although the sense of excitement we shared two weeks before had been replaced by a feeling of foreboding.

Once on the aircraft, we assumed our seats as they had been on the way out. I sat alone and the boys sat either side of Miriam. I was waiting for the next lunatic in my life to claim a seat next to me. Instead, a pretty, young, Italian girl took the window seat. I decided to ignore her.

Then we were at the destination airport. Next the long term car park and then the drive home in silence. No holiday reminiscences.

Miriam unpacked and went to bed. The boys went out to meet their friends. I was alone, but my thoughts would not leave me in peace. The television, the unconditional companion of the lonely, reminded me that it was Sunday. Good Christian folk sang their praises to the Lord hoping to be seen as good folk on the TV.

In just a fortnight, my vision of the Almighty had changed from an uncaring old man with a white beard to a sharing presence that was ignored by men. I could never understand why the creator of the Heaven and the Earth should want to sit on a golden throne, spending his days surrounded by sycophantic do-gooders who continually praised his works. I wondered what He thought of the televised congregation. Anyway, I am sure the source of everything has better things to do with Its time. Certainly, the scope and beauty of the Universe deserves to be praised, but the Almighty and the Universe must be the same thing.

We can sense the Spirit of everything that surrounds us. It seems only sensible to believe that the Universe can, and does, sense us. In order to experience what is there, however, we have to touch it. We have to feel part of it. Then we can ask for, and receive, help. In return, we must be prepared to give something back. Rather than building a dam to hold onto what should flow, we must allow everything to be shared and recycled. There is no magic for power but there is the magic of life. Misers hold onto misery as well as their money. Those that share goodness find that love is the true energy of the Universe. That is the love of all creation.

God is credited with creating man in his own image. No! Man created God in his own image for power and for deliverance from guilt when abhorrent crimes were, and are, committed in His name. The punch line is, of course, that He is the essence of everything. He is the planet, the plants and the animals. When we commit atrocities against the planet in the name of God then we commit all those crimes against the true God.

I flicked through the channels to find some news. After being away for a couple of weeks, I wanted to catch up. As I watched the story of the politician I had read about being explained and debated, the programme was interrupted to give a news flash about the San Andreas Fault showing signs of giving way. It was thought that masses of people could die. I watched as the updates came in way into the night before falling asleep in my chair.

The biggest issue seemed to be about what would happen to the Internet industries based in California. That is how cheap life has become.

CHAPTER FIFTEEN

ALARM BELLS

Monday

While the man was away, the snake slithered away from the pond. It had swallowed the last fish and basked in the sun wondering where its next meal would come from. When Godfrey returned from his holiday, he realised that everything had changed. Nature had destroyed his efforts. He had no other option than to break the remains up and start building again. This time, he would keep an eye on it to ensure that it developed as it should have done the first time.

I woke early in the morning, made my way to the bedroom and fell asleep until the alarm rang.

Miriam slept on. She had one more day of her holidays so she did not have to get up. The boys did not have school, so I showered, dressed and drove to my office, absorbed in the news coming from California.

Mary, a colleague who keeps my diary while I am away, went through the polite questions about my vacation, and I gave her the polite answers without mention of Annan, Lillie, the panic attacks or the onslaught on my spirituality.

I like to keep my appointments to a minimum when I return and there was nothing until ten-thirty. A new client, about whom Mary had written nothing. Her name was Jean Poole, a name that made me smile. Then one more person at noon.

At twenty-five minutes past ten, there was a knock on the door. 'Come in.' I was back at work. I turned my phone to the answering machine as usual.

My heart jumped as Lillie walked in. I froze for a moment. Then I motioned for her to sit down. I was silent. This crossroads had too many paths for me to choose a direction to travel in. My mind raced while my body froze.

'Hello, Gee. It's good to see you again.'

'And so soon.' I added, sarcastically, to make my mouth work. 'So, how can I help you?' I had reverted to my standard professional greeting. My mind added options. To compromise me again, to have my body for fun, to have my body for money, to apologise for what happened in Italy, to be Annan's messenger, to …'

'I need to explain a few things.' Lillie derailed my train of thought. 'I'll give you your session fee for listening.'

That was a strange thing to add. I was not going to be put into a position where my time was available to anybody for money. I was not a whore. I became assertive. 'If you have something of use to say, say it. I am a busy man and I have just lost the last two weeks of my life unravelling riddles that seemed to have nothing in them.'

'Annan needs you.' Lillie answered.

'Why? I am a clinical psychologist. I am not a user of women. I know nothing about business. I do not have contact with people of power who can be blackmailed.' My statement was designed to inform Lillie of Annan's business, if she had been unaware.

'You can be trusted. That is why.'

'So you want me to give up my practice and work in an illegal industry. Is that how my trustworthiness is viewed? And, anyway, why doesn't he ask me himself?'

'He will, if you will let him. Shall I call him so you can meet up?'

'No.' I replied. 'Give me his number and I will call him when I have done some thinking. Is that all now, or are you going to undress again?'

'Is that what you would like?'

I did not answer.

Lillie wrote Annan's number on a scrap of paper and handed it to me. Then she stood up and prepared to leave. She turned to me at the door and before she left, said, 'One day we will be on a friendlier footing than we are now. How much do I owe you for your time?' I waved her away with my hand and she left.

I turned my phone back on. No messages.

The time until my first proper appointment of the day was spent opening my mail and discarding the pile of junk that was sent to me on a very regular basis. How many trees are cut down in attempts to sell people stationery for people to send letters that will be discarded, to others?

My client was an old lady who was deaf. She could only understand me by reading my lips. 'How can I help you?' I asked, mouthing the words in an exaggerated way

She suffered from panic attacks. I wondered if she would accept laying on my floor with a book on her stomach. I decided against it and continued in the way I had for years.

After she left I phoned the number that Lillie had left. Annan answered. 'So you met my daughter again.'

I was stunned. Lillie was not the girl I had met many years before. My mind nudged me to remember to look up her notes. 'Your daughter! You have made your own child a prostitute. You bastard.'

Annan's voice raised in volume. 'She is not a prostitute. She is good at evaluating people, but she does not give or sell her body to anybody. She was working on testing your morality. She has no problem in being naked. She enjoys naturist holidays with her husband. You met him as well.'

I was stunned.

'Gee. I would like to meet up with you. I have a proposal for you.'

'When? I am busy.'

'How about now? I am having a coffee in a café near you.'

As a result of my own curiosity, I agreed, asked where he was and left my office.

As I walked into the cafe, Annan stood up and shook my hand. We sat down and he ordered two coffees.

'Let me explain about Lillie. She is my step-daughter. She is Jessie's child. She learnt about what we do from her mother and wanted to help. By the way, Jessie died a year ago from breast cancer. There was no way in which I let her sleep with the sort of people we target. Hypocritical as it sounds, I wanted her to retain her innocence. Well, now she susses out potential targets. If they show lascivious interest in her then they lack the moral fibre that people in authority should have. They lose the right to be left alone. Lillie deserves an Oscar, doesn't she?'

'So you deliberately target people who have power. That is so nasty.'

'No. we target people who abuse power for selfish gain and greed. Those people hurt to gain. They refuse to curb global warming in case they lose votes from the drivers of gas-guzzlers. They put profits before the alleviation of pain and suffering. They put building grand corporate headquarters before the repair of huts destroyed by earthquakes. And so on.

'There is no problem with hierarchies that use their size to help. There are plenty of them, but they are at risk from the pyramids of power in churches, governments and businesses. Somebody has to stand up to them. They are too powerful to fight with, but they are selfish enough to fall prey to the charms of girls and young men. Call me sick and then watch the television pictures of starving children in Africa. The collective conscience of the world wants to help them, but it is impotent. You saw the response to Live 8. The ordinary folk in the Western world are desperate to improve the lot of those who are hurting, yet the national interest in mineral rights, oil and the market for weapons in conflicts drags everybody's focus from the real issues of being humanitarian. When somebody gives a focus and a means, then people contribute.'

We were both quiet. We drank our coffees.

'So, how can I help you?' I then gave Annan the greeting I use with my clients.

'Some of the people who work for us need help. It is not an easy job to use your body to blackmail and coerce horrible men and women. They sometimes suffer from post traumatic stress. You treated my daughter many years ago. You brought her back to life after she discovered her mother in bed with two other men. She wanted to kill herself after the betrayal of every value she had. Her mother beat her because our daughter found out about her desire for dressing in rubber fetishist clothing and having sex with our friends' husbands. It sounds weird. After I found out about what had happened, I became very angry with my wife. She left me. I blamed myself for a long time. I had always had a bad temper and I thought our arguments had driven her into her strange sexual escapes.

'My daughter doesn't have contact with me because she

wants to forget all about those days. Perhaps you could address that issue as well for me, as well.'

I thought for a moment. 'And how much do I get paid?' I was embarrassed that I had asked.

Annan was ready for the question. 'Your normal fee and no more. That is the deal. And if I find that you have taken advantage of any of the girls then I will chop your balls off.' The look on his face made me take that threat at face value rather than as a joke.

We shook hands on the deal and agreed to review our progress in a month.

Annan asked me 'What do you think about the problems in America. The fault is another bell ringing on God's alarm clock. We can hear it. Will anybody else?'

The mention of impending disaster made me think.

'Here, Annan, I have a new client for you.' I said, handing him Roger's card as he left.

As I walked out, Lillie was standing outside. 'Annan has gone to get the car. He told me you have joined us. There is just one more thing. The scream you heard in Italy was not what you thought. Adam did not hit me. I found a lizard in the bed and I hate them. I screamed so loudly. Perhaps I need to see you. You treat phobias, don't you?'

'I think I need to think about that one.'

She kissed me on the cheek as I started to walk back to work.

Back at my office, I noticed that the little red light on my phone was flashing to tell me I had a message. I listened. It was Miriam.

'I want a divorce, Gee. It is easier to leave a message than to tell you face to face. Now you know. Now I have broken the ice, you can call me on my mobile. I am not at home.'

That was it. The end of my marriage on a message machine.

Even though I listened to it over and over, it was always the same.

I picked up the receiver and dialled Miriam's number. My heart was beating as fast as was possible without exploding. Adrenaline. I knew I had to keep my anger under control.

'Hello.' Miriam answered.

'Hi. It's Gee.'

'You are a bastard.' She told me. 'You screwed that blond bitch in the caravan next door, didn't you?'

Not only do we fight or run when threatened, we defend or freeze like a rabbit caught in car headlights. The latter two are passive reactions. I froze and thought about how I would protect myself.

How did she know? Yet I had done nothing anyway. I had been honey-trapped. I had no contact with her. No physical contact, anyway.

I had to find out what, and who, had told Miriam this false information.

'What the hell are you talking about? I have done nothing. I screwed nobody apart from you on that holiday.'

That little voice, Freud's super-ego, started to chatter to me. Why had I used the word 'screw' when referring to our lovemaking? Why had I implied that I had screwed others before we went on holiday?

Miriam was silent for a moment and then she exploded. 'I came to your office and saw her leaving. How long have you two been seeing each other?'

'She came to see me with a message from Annan. He wanted to meet me.'

'So why didn't he phone you to make an appointment? Why did he send the floozy? And how does he know her anyway? They never met in Italy.'

'Miriam. Can we meet up and talk? I have done nothing wrong and you have got the wrong end of the stick.'

'I'll think about it. I'll call you later.' Miriam hung up.

When I called back her phone had been turned off.

Adam and Eve had found something to argue about that was as fundamental as Eve eating the apple. Now it was me who had been accused of committing a sin, yet I was as innocent as Eve had been. Now I was being kicked out of the Eden of my life, I had sold my soul, somehow, to a stranger on the day that God's wake up call rang so loudly that the earth in California shook again. It was Monday, the day after the day of rest.

I had a lot of explaining to do with Miriam.

Printed in the United Kingdom
by Lightning Source UK Ltd.
110145UKS00001B/211-246